DEAR KAREN

Dear Bobby: I need help. I'm in love with this girl, but she doesn't even know I exist. I can't seem to come up with a way to tell her how I feel.
Signed: Hopeful

I chewed on my pen while I tried to come up with an answer.

Dear Hopeful, I wrote. You have to do something to make her notice you. Sounds to me as if you might just be too shy or quiet or ordinary right now. You're going to have to take chances. Find out what would impress her. No girl can resist a romantic hero. – Bobby

I passed it across to Adam.

His cheeks turned pink as he read, but he passed it back and made an "OK" sign.

At the end of class he stood beside me as I put my binder into my bag. "Uh, Karen, I've been thinking," he said. "Maybe we could go for coffee or ice-cream after school today. I'd really like to talk to you, somewhere away from this place . . ."

Janet Quin-Harkin was born in Bath and educated in England, Austria and Germany. She studied dance and drama as a child and went straight from college to work for the BBC, where she wrote several plays.

Yearning for sunshine she went to Australia to work for Australian Broadcasting. Within weeks she was given a contract to draw a daily cartoon for the *Australian* newspaper. In Sydney she met her husband. The Quin-Harkins moved to California, where they lived for twenty years and raised four children.

Janet Quin-Harkin began writing children's books when living in San Francisco. Her first picture book, *Peter Penny's Dance*, won many awards, including *The New York Times* Best Book of the Year Award. She has subsequently written more than fifty books for young adults.

Janet Quin-Harkin is now a full-time writer and also teaches creative writing at a nearby college.

Dear Karen

Also available in the Boyfriend Club series

the boyfriend club

12

club

Dear Karen

JANET QUIN-HARKIN

PUFFIN BOOKS

PUFFIN BOOKS

Published by the Penguin Group
Penguin Books Ltd, 27 Wrights Lane, London W8 5TZ, England
Penguin Books USA Inc., 375 Hudson Street, New York, New York 10014, USA
Penguin Books Australia Ltd, Ringwood, Victoria, Australia
Penguin Books Canada Ltd, 10 Alcorn Avenue, Toronto, Ontario, Canada M4V 3B2
Penguin Books (NZ) Ltd, 182–190 Wairau Road, Auckland 10, New Zealand

Penguin Books Ltd, Registered Offices: Harmondsworth, Middlesex, England

First published 1995
1 3 5 7 9 10 8 6 4 2

Produced by Daniel Weiss Associates Inc.,
33 West 17th Street, New York, NY 10011, USA

The moral right of the author has been asserted

Made and printed in England by Clays Ltd, St Ives plc

To my English fans

Chapter

1

Alta Mesa High, September 20. Chemistry I class. Latest scoop from your on-the-spot reporter, Karen Nguyen. After a very rocky start to the new school year, the Boyfriend Club is now back in full swing. No great disasters if you don't count several minor incidents—like Justine almost moving to England, Roni almost transferring to some school in the boonies, me almost going to the music conservatory, and Ginger's cousin Lacey making her life miserable. Oh, and Ginger and Roni not speaking to each other because of a major fight over Josh White and the sophomore presidential election.

Everything is going great now, though, apart from the fact that Owen, leader of the nerd pack, beat out both Ginger and Roni to become president

*of the sophomore class. AND my parents are mad
at me for dropping out of the music conservatory.
AND a creepy nerd called Jeremy has followed me
all the way from music camp to Alta Mesa. AND
he's still crazy about me, but Justine's crazy about
him and popular sophomore Josh is crazy about
Ginger but Roni's crazy about him and Ginger's
still not sure about Ben and . . .*

I stopped. Not the greatest news sentences.
News should be short and snappy. I chewed at the
end of my pen. Bad habit, I know, but it helps me
think. Anyway, one bad habit isn't bad. I think perfect people are boring, don't you?

Speaking of boring people, Mr. Parnow, in
whose chemistry class I was now suffering, could
easily win the award for Most Boring Teacher in
the Universe, no contest. Chemistry classes go like
this: "Regarding molecules blah blah blah and fur-
thermore research during the late nineteenth cen-
tury has shown blah blah blah. . . ." You see what I
mean? Even if he was saying something world shat-
tering, the way he says it, in that monotonous voice,
makes me switch off.

Which was why I was practicing writing news
stories instead of taking notes. You're probably surprised that I'm the one fooling around in class. I
know—usually I'm the good student of the group.
I'm the one who always has my three-by-five cards

to help me study for finals. I always have my home-work turned in on time. Justine calls me Miss Goody Two-Shoes. I don't really want to be, but I was brought up that way. I have very strict parents, for one thing. They came from Vietnam, where you let down a whole bunch of ancestors if you don't do well in school. They never let me even breathe be-fore my homework is done, and they have heart at-tacks if I don't get all A's.

They even sent me to a strict Catholic girls school, until it became too expensive and they transferred me to Alta Mesa High. Those terrifying teachers at the Catholic school didn't give me a chance to goof off. They walked around the class-room, swinging rulers dangerously close to our hands. And heaven help anyone who was passing notes, doodling, or sinning in some other way.

So I'd been very well behaved right until I started Alta Mesa. After a whole year of Roni, Ginger, and Justine, though, I was finally able to loosen up. I'd passed notes, whispered in class, and become normal. But now I was running the risk of flunking chemistry. Not that I wanted to flunk—I just couldn't understand what Mr. Parnow was try-ing to say.

I looked down at my news item. It wasn't really for a newspaper. Our Boyfriend Club wasn't big enough to have its own newspaper. There were only four members, and we saw each other every day. I was just practicing, actually. Our first editorial staff meeting of the *Alta Mesa Heights,* our school newspaper, was after school today and I wanted to make sure that I didn't spend another year as the gopher. (You know . . . Go for this and go for that. Get it?)

I'd only joined the newspaper staff toward the end of last school year, and only to get close to senior superstar Damien Evans, so I hadn't minded too much that my biggest assignment had been to clean out the newsroom closet. Now that I was a mature sophomore, I wanted to be a real reporter, or have my own column with my own name on it. But I wasn't sure where I'd be able to find my own little niche. All the good assignments already would have been snapped up by upper-class students. I wasn't a jock, so they wouldn't use me as a sports reporter. A very snobby junior called Gabrielle was the news editor and I knew she had a whole clique of followers who would get the juicy news stories. Which didn't leave much for someone at the bottom, like me.

What I definitely didn't want was to spend another year scraping unidentifiable pieces of moldy sandwich from the closet floor. I wanted to feel that I was part of the newspaper, at the hub of activity, getting the pulse of school life, right there for any breaking story.

I also wanted to prove that I could do stuff other than music.

That's why I was trying out different writing styles now, to see what I could do best. They didn't have a gossip columnist. Maybe I really could do that, except that I only knew gossip about my close friends. It wasn't as if I was popular and involved in a lot of activities. But I had to be good at something. . . .

If only Damien had still been editor, I know he would have let me do some real writing. Damien had been last year's editor, as well as the cutest guy in the school. We'd actually gone on a date once— well, it was almost a date. We'd been to a coffee-house together and sat talking all evening. It was the most special evening of my life. Something I'd never forget, anyway.

Damien had promised me my own series of articles on runaway teens last year, but he'd graduated before it could happen.

"Which draws us to the conclusion that the substance has to be . . . what?" I looked up, hearing the question in Mr. Parnow's voice. His eyes were directly on me. "You, Karen . . . Nguyen. What substance can we expect to find at this point on the periodic table?"

I stared at him in horror. I hated being called on, even when I did know the answer. I'm kind of

shy about speaking up with everyone watching me.
But I hate looking like a fool even more. I felt my
heart pounding. How could I say that I didn't have
a clue what he was talking about? Had he been
watching my doodling and known that I wasn't
paying attention?

I looked around the room for help. How come
none of my friends were in this class? Ginger and Roni
were taking chemistry, but not the same period and
not the same teacher. Lucky them. Across from me I
caught the eye of Adam, my fellow gopher on the
school newspaper, his mop of unruly black curls bob-
bing above heavy-rimmed glasses and big dark eyes.

He pointed to the third finger on his left hand,
then held it up proudly. I couldn't imagine what he
was doing. Had he totally flipped? He wasn't wearing a ring or anything. He looked at me and made a
face as if he were excited and happy. He was still
waving that finger. Something began to click in my
brain. Ring? Engagement ring? Ring made of gold?
No, gold wasn't right. He was pointing to something
in the ring. Diamond . . . and diamonds are . . .
"Carbon?" I stammered.

Mr. Parnow nodded. "Correct. The element is
carbon."

I sat back with a huge sigh of relief.

"Thanks," I mouthed to Adam. He grinned and
gave me a thumbs-up sign.

After that I didn't dare try out my skills as gossip columnist. I stared at Mr. Parnow, trying to pay attention as he droned on. Luckily the bell rang soon after.

"Thanks for saving my life there," I said to Adam as we collected our books.

He smiled shyly. "You caught on pretty quickly."

"I was desperate," I said. "I can't understand a thing that man says."

Adam nodded. "Me either. I try to concentrate really hard so I can understand what he's saying, but I keep nodding off to sleep. I'm scared that I'm going to start snoring one of these days."

"I'll nudge you if you do," I said. "One good turn deserves another."

"Thanks," Adam said. "Are you going to the newspaper meeting after school?"

"Yes, are you?"

He nodded. "See you there."

"Sure," I said. "I hope I get something to do this year. Last year I felt like a slave."

"Me, too. They had me clean out the closet and sweep the trash off the floor all year."

"They had *you* clean up for them? I thought nobody had touched that closet for a hundred years. I found food with things growing on it."

Adam laughed. "I found it, too, but I just kicked it farther into the corner where nobody could see it."

"Thanks a lot. I was the one who had to sweep out that corner."

We walked out of the classroom and joined the crowd flowing down the hall.

"See you later," Adam said.

"See you later."

As I hurried to my locker I realized something—Adam had actually spoken to me. I had joined the newspaper last spring and I'd seen Adam at meetings, but I didn't recall that he'd ever said a word to anyone. I'd thought he was super shy—even shyer than me, if that was possible. He'd turned bright red when anyone spoke to him and always sat there as if he wanted to blend in with the furniture.

Actually Adam had been a skinny little kid then, a likely candidate for the nerd pack. (That's what we call this group of dweeby guys who are always bugging us. More about them later.) But he grew a few inches during the summer, and he'd filled out rather nicely. Those dark curls were interesting—a little like my old boyfriend James's hair, but way curlier.

Come to think of it, Adam didn't look bad at all.

Chapter

2

I grabbed my lunch bag and went to meet my friends under our favorite tree. Let me just say that sane people don't go outside in Phoenix in September. The temperature is still hot enough to melt metal. Alta Mesa has a perfectly good air-conditioned cafeteria, if you like fighting three thousand kids for a seat at a table and you can stand a billion decibels of noise level, not to mention being struck in the back of the neck by a flying tortilla.

We'd started eating lunch under a big cottonwood tree when we were all new students at Alta Mesa. By now it had become a Boyfriend Club tradition, and we liked it, even when it was broiling outside.

I grinned to myself as I came around the corner

and saw Roni dumping her book bag under our tree. Before I could reach her, Justine and Ginger arrived from the other direction.

"That's it. I quit," Justine said, throwing down her bag in disgust.

"Quit what?" Ginger asked, sitting down beside Roni in the shade.

"School, of course."

"Why, what's the problem?" I asked. I opened my lunch bag and spread out my sandwich, peach, and granola bar on my napkin.

Justine made a face. "Lots of things, especially geometry," she hissed. "Nobody told me that sophomore year was going to be hard."

"Geometry's not so bad," I said.

She looked at me as if I were a creature from another planet. "Not so bad? It's terrible, Karen. Who was this Pythagoras guy, anyway, and how do we know he was right? How come he has nothing better to do than make up stupid theorems? What good is it going to do me to prove that one line is longer than another when I can already see that it is? I wish I could drop math," Justine said. "I'll never understand it."

"I feel the same way about chemistry," I said. "I just can't understand that Mr. Parnow."

The others looked surprised. "*You* can't understand? Karen the superbrain?" Justine teased.

18

"Even I can understand so far," Ginger said. "And I'm not the greatest science person."

"You don't have Mr. Parnow," I said. "He's impossible! He's so boring that I just can't pay attention to what he's saying, no matter how important it is. When he called on me today, I wouldn't have known what he was asking, except that a boy helped me."

"Ooohhh, Karen got helped by a boy!" Justine teased.

"Shut up." I laughed. "It's only this guy who's on the newspaper with me. Remember the freshman guy called Adam I told you about last year—the one who blushed when anyone spoke to him?"

"Isn't your first meeting today?"

I nodded. "After school. The new editor hands out assignments. I hope I get to write something. I'm going to quit if I'm a gopher again."

"Who's the new editor?"

"Brad Smith," I said. "Kind of serious looking, with longish dark hair."

"Gee, what a letdown after Damien." Justine sighed. "He was something else. I still think you should have done more about your relationship with him, Karen. He might have asked you to his senior prom."

"In my dreams," I said. "Face it, Justine. Damien was a senior and I was a very ordinary little

19

freshperson. He was just being friendly because I helped him with his brother. Guys like that don't date girls like me." I paused and took a big bite of turkey sandwich. "Come to think of it," I said, "guys of any kind are rather scarce in my life right now."

"You can say that again," Roni agreed. "We must be the only Boyfriend Club in the world with no boyfriends."

"Ginger has a boyfriend," Justine said.

Ginger made a face. "Sometimes I wonder," she said. "Even though I know Ben loves me, I think he's more in love with football right now than he is with me. He sure spends more time at practice. And when he does stop by my house, he's so tired he falls asleep on my sofa!"

"That's what happens when you date the star wide receiver," Roni said.

Ginger sighed. "Sometimes I think I'd rather have a normal boyfriend who wasn't a star and who made time for me," she said. "I'm beginning to think that a whole year of dating the same guy is long enough."

"Ginger!" Justine exclaimed. "You're not seriously thinking of dropping Ben?"

"I'm thinking about cooling off for a while," Ginger said. "Maybe agreeing to see other people."

"You wouldn't care if Ben dated other people?" I asked.

Ginger sighed again. "Yes, I would. I don't know what I want. I'm just fed up with sitting home on weekends while Ben is off with the football team."

"At least you have a guy who notices you exist," Justine said. "I've been trying to get Jeremy to notice me, but all he does is gaze at Karen."

"If there's anything I can do to help Jeremy notice you, believe me, I'll do it," I said. "I can't understand what you could possibly see in him. He's such a dweeb!"

"I think he's romantic looking," Justine said. "So dark and brooding . . . sort of like Johnny Depp, with glasses and a bow tie." She paused as I spluttered at this description, then suddenly dug me in the ribs excitedly. "Look, there he is now!"

"Not again? Where?" I got ready to run.

"Standing in the doorway, watching us. I'm sure it's Jeremy." Then she grabbed me again. "Yes, and look, he's coming over, Karen!"

I watched as Jeremy came down the path toward us. He was wearing a black shirt and black pants, and with that longish dark hair he looked like a young Dracula, nerd style. I had no idea why Justine found him romantic looking. Creepy was more like it.

I guess I should explain that I met Jeremy at music camp in Colorado this summer. I didn't hate him at first. He wasn't bad looking, for one thing.

21

He has shoulder-length hair and a thin, hungry-looking face—he might make a good rock star if he wasn't so neat and clean and boring. I mean, he always wore a bow tie at camp, he polished his shoes *every* day, and his idea of fun dinner conversation was quoting statistics!

Unfortunately Jeremy had to develop a monster crush on me. Every time I sat down, he sat next to me. If I went for a walk, he was right there behind me. Sometimes I'd get the spooky feeling that someone was watching me, and it was Jeremy, just sitting there and staring at me.

By the end of the first week he was driving me crazy. If I tried to talk to him, all he wanted to do was talk about classical music, and he was so intense about it that it scared me. I guess I didn't want to be reminded that I'd have to be intense about my music someday if I wanted to be a professional violinist, which was my parents' dream for me.

I thought I'd seen the last of him when the bus drove away from camp, but then his father got transferred to Phoenix and he begged to go to Alta Mesa to be with me again. Imagine how bummed he must have been when he got here and found that I'd enrolled at the music conservatory instead. It only took me three days to admit what I'd known all along—that I didn't belong at the music conservatory. And what do you think the first thing

I found when I came back to Alta Mesa was? Jeremy, waiting for me with a big, hopeful smile on his face. Yuck!

And here he was, right in front of me. "Hi, Karen," he said softly as he took a step closer.

"Hi," I muttered. I was desperately thinking of some way to say, "Jeremy, meet Justine. Justine, meet Jeremy. Bye." But my brain always went into panic mode when he was around, so I kept my mouth shut.

"Remember that song I wrote for you?" he asked in his deep, nasal voice. "I really want to hear you play it for me on the violin. Maybe we could perform it as a duet. Don't you think it would sound great?"

My problem is that I find it hard to be rude, even to people I don't like. Roni or Justine or Ginger would have told him to get lost, but I found myself mumbling, "I haven't had time to practice it yet."

"Promise me you will someday," Jeremy said. "Please play it once for me, Karen. And if you don't like it, I'll write you another one."

"I'm in the middle of lunch with my friends right now, Jeremy," I said.

He took the hint and sighed loudly before he walked on.

"Now do you see what he's like?" I asked my friends. "Do normal boys go around wanting to play duets with you?"

Justine sighed, too. "I'd love him to make up a song for me. That is so romantic."

"Anyway, what are we going to do about finding new guys for ourselves?" Roni demanded, bringing our conversation back to important matters. "It's a new school year. We need four new cute, adorable, smart, and caring guys, right?"

"Who look like Johnny Depp, Brad Pitt, Luke Perry, and Jason Priestley," Justine said, waving a carrot stick excitedly.

"Yeah, right, at this school?" I laughed. "Right now I'd settle for any guy who wasn't Jeremy."

I broke off. A squeaky voice was yelling at us from the other end of the path. "Howdy, girls! It's us. Your dreamboats are coming!"

"I take that back," I yelled.

We tried to scramble to our feet, but it was too late. Nerds were coming down the path in our direction. Our only way of escape was blocked. There were tall, skinny ones; short, shrimpy ones; and one very large one. That was Wolfgang, the blimpy nerd with the mismatched clothing. Usually I don't care what people wear. I'm not like Justine, who looks down on anyone who isn't designer coordinated. But Wolfgang was too much even for me. I mean, orange-and-neon-green surfer pants, topped by a giant stars-and-stripes T-shirt. I wished I'd remembered my sunglasses.

24

But he wasn't even the most repulsive nerd. Ronald was wearing shorts—short, baby-blue shorts that exposed his knobby knees.

"Just the girls we were looking for, right, guys?" Owen asked. I was about to say squeaked, but his voice had miraculously changed recently. He'd grown, too, from a shrimpy nerd into a skinny one. He actually looked okay now, apart from the pocket protector in his shirt pocket, but changing his personality wasn't going to be so easy. To think that he was our class president!

Owen grinned his repulsive grin about an inch from my face. "Here she is, the young lady we have to talk to."

"Me?" This time I squeaked. Being that close to Owen was too much for any normal human to bear.

"You, you wicked person," Owen said.

"Me? What have I done?"

"Only broken our friend Jeremy's heart," Owen said. "You spurned him again, didn't you? Well, we're going to help him win you back."

"Win me back? I was never his in the first place." I didn't know whether to laugh or cry. I was enclosed in a circle of nerdy faces, all glaring at me accusingly.

"He came all the way from Colorado to be close to you, Karen, and now you do nothing but break his heart."

"Give me a break, Owen," I said. "His parents were transferred here from Colorado. You make it sound like he came here alone in a covered wagon."

"I bet he would have, if he hadn't persuaded his parents to move," Owen said seriously.

I held up my hand. "Look, guys, I'm really sorry, but I can't help it if Jeremy isn't the guy for me," I said.

Justine coughed in my ear and kicked my ankle.

"On the other hand," I said, "Justine is just dying to get to know Jeremy better. Why don't you work on that?"

"Jeremy and Justine?" Ronald demanded. "Don't be ridiculous! Jeremy is smart and intellectual and quite cultured. Justine is an airhead. No offense, Justine, but your idea of culture is seeing the Pocahontas exhibit at the mall."

Justine looked as if she was about to hit him. "Shut up, you little creep. I'm cultured," she yelled. "I'll have you know that I've been to Paris. I've seen the Mona Lisa. Or at least I think I have. Is she the one with the missing arm?"

"That proves my point," Ronald said. "You and Jeremy have absolutely nothing in common. Besides, he wants Karen, and he's not going to rest until he gets her."

Owen made a sweeping gesture. "We have delivered our message. Now you know, Karen. Jeremy will do what it takes to win your heart, and we're going to help him. Be warned. Come on, guys, the computer lab is calling."

"I don't hear anything," we heard Wolfgang mumble as they hurried away.

I was still pressed against the tree trunk in a state of shock when Roni chuckled. "It's okay, Karen, you can relax. They're gone."

"You guys might have helped me," I complained. "You let me get pinned against a tree by nerds."

Justine still looked mad. "All you need to do is find a way to make Jeremy like me," she said. "Then you won't have any more problems."

"I'll work on it," I said. "In fact, we'll get the Boyfriend Club to work on it. It can be our first real assignment of the school year—get Justine and Jeremy together, whatever it takes."

"That's simple," Roni said. "We just have to turn Justine into a music whiz and all-around brain."

"I know music," Justine said. "I don't know why everyone seems to think I'm such an airhead. I've been to concerts all over the world. That's it— maybe Jeremy will be impressed when he hears that I went to a concert in London, in Hyde Park! I must see if I've still got the program so that I can impress him by remembering what they played. Wasn't it Beethoven's *1812 Overture*?" Her face lit up. "And I could take up an instrument, couldn't I?

27

What instrument is easiest to learn—say in a month?"

"Triangle, Justine," Ginger said dryly.

Justine's eyes flashed. "I want to impress him, not amuse him. I want a real instrument."

"Justine, you can't learn any instrument in a month," I said. "A few chords on the guitar, maybe."

"But I want to play in the orchestra," Justine said. "I'm going to see the music teacher and find out what they're short of. Then I'll get my dad to pay for private lessons. You wait—we'll see who's cultured. Jeremy will definitely be impressed."

I caught Roni winking at me and I tried not to laugh. Justine always came up with the wildest schemes and something always seemed to go wrong. But she never stopped trying. I had to admire that. I had to admire her confidence, too. I'd been studying violin for eleven years now and Justine thought she could be good enough for an orchestra in a month. I only wished she would be. There was nothing I wanted more than Jeremy out of my hair!

Chapter

3

I spent the afternoon seriously thinking about ways to get Jeremy and Justine together. It wasn't going to be easy. Jeremy was a musical and intellectual snob. He'd been critical of students at music camp who weren't as good as he was. Imagine what he'd think if he discovered that Justine thought the Beatles were classical! But I'd do pretty much anything to get Jeremy out of my life—I was even considering giving Justine a hurried course of violin lessons!

Luckily, thinking about Justine and Jeremy helped me not to worry too much about what was going to happen at that first newspaper staff meeting, which I was going to be late for if I didn't hurry. I felt excited and scared at the same time. I loved the idea of working on the newspaper, being at the place where it was all happening, writing scoops. But I was scared that I wouldn't have the guts to speak up if I wasn't given a real assignment.

I jumped when someone tapped me on the shoulder and said, "I hope you're not ignoring me on purpose." I spun around and saw that it was Adam.

"Oh, hi, Adam," I said guiltily. "Sorry. I was miles away."

"Planning your speech to convince Brad to make you head news writer, or still trying to conquer chemistry?"

I grinned. "Not even close," I said. "If you really want to know, I'm trying to figure out a way to get one of my best friends together with a guy she likes. It's not going to be easy because they're total opposites."

"You think that works—meddling in other people's lives?"

I looked away, embarrassed. "It's not really meddling, is it? I'm just trying to be helpful." I stopped and tried not to grin. Helpful to myself, too, but I didn't add that. I just went on. "Sometimes outsiders can see things more clearly and give helpful hints. It's worked before for my friends."

A big grin spread across his face. "Oh, that's right. I remember hearing something about it last year. Don't you guys have a boyfriend club? Like a matchmaking service?"

I tried to laugh it off. "It's not really a club—it only started as a joke, and we certainly don't run a matchmaking service. Not for other people, anyway. It's just like I said—sometimes a person observing from the outside can see ways to solve problems."

"More like an advice service, then?"

"You make it sound so official. It's just my friends and I, helping each other survive high school."

Adam nodded. "Sounds okay to me. That's what friends are for, isn't it?"

"You certainly saved my life in chemistry class this morning," I said. "I thought I was going to die when Mr. Parnow called on me."

"You can return the favor sometime," he said casually as we approached the door of the newspaper office.

There were voices coming from inside, talking and laughing loudly. Adam and I both hesitated in the hallway.

Adam looked at me. "Okay, ready to get in there and demand our rights? We're not picking up one more piece of moldy food, and we want good writing assignments!"

I gave him a nervous grin. "I'm not looking forward

to this. I'm not very good at demanding my rights."

"Neither am I," he said. "I sort of freeze up when people look at me. I plan great sentences to say, but when I open my mouth, nothing will come out and I hear myself stammering like an idiot."

"Same with me," I said.

He nodded. "It's tough being shy. You can never say what you want to people."

"You don't seem to have a problem talking with me," I pointed out.

"You're different. You're not threatening like most people."

"Is that good or bad?"

"What do you mean?"

"Either you see me as sweet and gentle or as a wimp."

"Definitely sweet and gentle."

"Thanks," I said. "I guess we should get in there before they start without us."

"After you," he said with a gracious bow.

"Coward." We grinned at each other as we went in.

There were about a dozen people sitting around the table in the office and they looked up as we came in.

"Hi, there," Brad said politely. "I know you two from last year. It's Kim, isn't it?"

"Karen," I said.

"Oh, Karen, right. And you're?"

"Adam."

"Adam. Hi. Welcome. You know everyone else, don't you? Gabrielle is going to be our news editor, so most of you will be working for her."

I looked across at Gabrielle. "Hi," I said.

I knew right away that she wasn't my favorite sort of person. Even last year, when she'd been a sophomore nobody, she'd ignored me and spent all her time flirting with Damien and the senior guys. Her blond hair was spiral permed, making it into a huge mane of untamed curls that cascaded over her shoulders. She had very wide baby-blue eyes and very red lips and she was wearing a blue denim halter top and white shorts.

She sort of half smiled back at Adam and me and half raised her hand to say hi. I got the feeling she thought we weren't worth any more than that. She was a junior big shot and acting like it.

"I guess we should get started," Brad said. "Let's get our department teams firmed up, then we can discuss copy for the first edition, which comes out next week, in case you've forgotten."

He looked around the room. "Steve is going to be our sports editor. Have you got all the staff you need, Steve?"

I recognized Steve. He was a basketball star, so it made sense to put him in charge of sports. "Uh . . . sure, I think we've got everything covered," he said.

"I've got Tom doing football, Ginny doing girls volleyball, Pete doing soccer . . . yeah, I'd say we're okay." All the people he had named were jocks. They'd already established their own little clique. Not that I wanted to do sports anyway, but it wouldn't have made any difference if I had.

"And you say you're fine, Gabrielle?" Brad asked. He gave her a little smile as if he wanted to let her know that he thought she was fine, in more ways than one.

She picked up on the smile. "Sure. Everything under control," she purred back. "We've got so many great writers returning from last year that we're in great shape. I think we're going to get some fabulous stuff. This is going to be one hot newspaper."

I could feel my throat getting tighter. Any minute now I'd find that all the jobs were taken and it would be back to cleaning the closet.

"Uh . . . excuse me a second," I blurted. I could feel all the eyes in the room on me. "I don't have an assignment yet and neither does Adam. We both joined in the middle of last year and we never really got assigned to any department."

"Except cleaning the closet," Adam added.

This got a laugh.

"And I take it you're not volunteering for closet cleaning again?" Brad asked with a smile. "What department do you think you'd like to work in?"

I wanted to say news, but I didn't want to be turned down flat by Gabrielle. I also didn't want her to feel that she had to take me and then only give me broken vending machines and teacher retirements to report on.

"I . . . really wouldn't have any work for an extra person," Gabrielle said quickly. "We're pretty much a close-knit team in news."

Okay, so she'd made that clear enough. I was feeling mad now as well as embarrassed. If only Damien was here, I thought. Damien, the most popular guy in the school, who had kissed me once and told me that I was special, and who had wanted me to work with him on a special feature on runaway kids. . . .

"I'd kind of like to work on special features," I said. "Last year Damien wanted me to do a report on runaway kids with him. It's just that he never had time to get it started."

"Damien never had time for anything," Gabrielle said, tossing back all those blond curls. "Well, he had time for some things. . . ." Gabrielle continued, blushing as if she'd been involved in some of those things with him. "Talk about an overloaded life. Was there anything he wasn't involved in?"

"Runaway kids?" Brad was nodding seriously. "Yeah, something like that might be interesting later in the year. Right now we have to concentrate on getting the paper set up with regular columns. One of the things I want to do as editor this year is make the paper more fun, so that more kids will actually want to read it. I'd like to have a question-of-the-month column—you know, where someone goes around campus asking people how they feel about something in the news. And maybe a gossip column. Last year was too serious—great for winning journalism awards, but not great for keeping readers interested. We're a high school paper. We should be fun."

I knew this was my big chance. If I spoke up quickly, I might even get my own column. But I couldn't decide whether I'd ever have the nerve to be the question person and go around campus interviewing people, or whether I could really write a successful gossip column. A little voice in my head was whispering that I couldn't do either well enough. I guess I'm vain, but I hate doing something I can't do well.

My palms were sweaty, my forehead was clammy. *Go on, say something, dummy, before it's too late,* I was commanding myself.

Then I heard Adam's voice beside me. "You should get Karen to do an advice column. You know, the Dear Abby of Alta Mesa."

"An advice column?" Brad was nodding again.

"That's not a bad idea. And is Karen a whiz at giving advice?"

"She's had a lot of experience helping her friends sort out personal problems," Adam said.

"That's right, I remember now." Brad was looking at me as if I'd turned into an interesting person. "I heard about how you helped Damien with his little brother last year. Good thinking, Adam." He paused. "So what about it, Karen? Would you like to do an advice column? Do you think that's something you could handle?"

I took a deep breath. "I'd like to try," I said.

"Great," Brad said. "Why don't you write me some sample questions and answers? I imagine you'd have to write the first couple of columns yourself anyway, before you got any real people writing in with problems."

"Okay, great, I'll do that," I said. I was trying not to grin, trying to look like a person who got great assignments every day of her life.

"She'll need a name," one of the girls said. "You know, like Dear Abby."

"How about Dear Aunty Karen," one of the boys suggested.

Everyone groaned. "That sounds so prissy and old fashioned," Gabrielle said. "We want something snappy."

"I have an idea," I said. I was thinking about

Roni's name and how they enrolled her in guys PE by mistake. "What about something like Dear Bobby? Then it could be a boy or a girl who is giving the advice."

"That's good," Brad said. "Dear Bobby. I like that, Karen. I think this is going to work out great."

"Shouldn't we get started on planning now?" Gabrielle asked. "We've wasted enough time and I have to be home by five-thirty."

"Heavy date, Gaby?" asked Steve, the sports editor.

"None of your business," Gabrielle snapped, "and my name's Gabrielle."

I got the feeling there was a current going between those two, and it wasn't positively charged.

"Okay," Brad said hastily. "Let's talk about what our first lead story should be."

Everyone launched right into a discussion of what the hot news topics around school were. I was still in a state of shock about getting my own column and wondering if I could really handle it, so I sat there, listening to everyone talking. Suddenly something occurred to me—Adam didn't have a job. He'd spoken up for me. I should have done the same for him.

I leaned across to him. "You don't have anything yet," I whispered.

"I know. It's okay."

"No, it's not. You should have said something

before they went on. You spoke up for me. Do you want me to remind Brad for you?"

He shook his head firmly. "It's okay. I'll talk to him later."

"But you could have had a column, too."

He shook his head again. All those wild curls danced. "I couldn't do what he wanted. I'd never have the nerve to go up to people and question them. They'd tell me to get lost."

"Adam! Stop being so defeatist." I thought I was shy and modest, but I was pushy compared to him.

He held up his hand to me. "I'll handle it later, Karen. Thanks for the offer. I'm glad you got what you wanted."

At the end of the session I almost pushed him. "Adam, go talk to Brad now. Tell him what you want to do."

Adam laughed nervously. "You're bossy, did you know that?"

"If you don't talk to him, I'll throw more sandwiches into the back of the closet for you to clean up," I threatened.

"Okay, okay. I'll talk to him."

I watched as he stood there waiting for Brad to be free. It took a long while. Then I realized that I had no excuse for hanging around. It was like snooping and I had no right to pry into Adam's life. Besides, I had to go home and get working on my first real column. All I had to do was think up my own questions and answer them. What could be simpler? I had a big, happy smile on my face as I left the room. I was Dear Bobby. I had my own column. I couldn't wait to tell Roni and Ginger and Justine.

It was funny that I was thinking about telling them at that moment, because Brad ran after me and grabbed my arm. "Wait up a second, Karen. I just remembered something," he said.

I stopped, scared that he might say he'd changed his mind and I wasn't going to be Dear Bobby after all.

"You can't let anyone know who you are," Brad said. "You have to be the mysterious, elusive Dear Bobby." He looked around at the others. "The same goes for all of you. Don't blab and give away the identity of Dear Bobby, understand?"

"That's right," Gabrielle said to her friend Margie, loudly enough for me to hear. "Who'd want her advice if they knew? After all, she's only a boring little sophomore. What can she possibly know about life?"

So the feeling was mutual. She disliked me as much as I disliked her. In one day I'd made a friend and an enemy.

Chapter 4

The house was quiet as I let myself in that afternoon. Okay, so my house is always quiet. I never know whether my parents are home or not. They don't have the radio or TV blasting like most people do. In fact, they hardly watch TV at all. My mother says there's too much violence and the news is always bad.

"Mom?" I called. "Are you home?"

"In the kitchen," she called back.

She was never anywhere else. That was one of the things that bugged me about my family—everything was always the same. Every afternoon she was there in the kitchen and she'd have a glass of milk and two cookies waiting for me. We always ate the same things for dinner—mostly Vietnamese and never hamburger. Nothing in the house was ever out of place. It was too quiet and way too boring.

I found myself wishing, as I'd done so many times before, that I had a sister or even a little brother, like Roni. It was so hard being an only child. All my parents' energy concentrated on me. If I sneezed, I had pneumonia and I was immediately rushed to bed with hot water bottles. If I scratched a mosquito bite, I had chicken pox—no, make that smallpox. It was always something seriously dramatic. Roni or Ginger could be sick for days and nobody would even notice.

Even Justine had a baby sister now—and such a cute baby sister at that. I thought about how wonderful it would be to have a baby sister like Alexandra, who smiled and cooed whenever I went near her. But there was no use talking to my mom about it. Every time I asked her why she didn't have any more children, she launched into this big lecture on how much it cost to raise a child and to pay for violin lessons and how it was going to take all their savings to put just one child through college.

I dropped my book bag onto the hall floor and took a deep breath before I went through to the kitchen.

"Hi, Mom." I gave her a kiss on the cheek. She stood there like a statue and didn't try to kiss me back. Neither of my parents is big on hugs.

"How was your day?" she asked.

"Great," I said. "Guess what? We had our first newspaper meeting today, and I've been given my own column to write."

She sniffed as she placed the cookies in front of me. "So now you have even less time for violin practice," she said. "Your father and I, we think we have wasted all that money on your violin lessons for nothing. You have such a talent, too. You had a chance to go to the conservatory where only the very best go, and instead you choose to write for a newspaper."

My parents had been so excited when I was offered a scholarship to the Phoenix Conservatory of Music this fall. I'd tried to be excited, too. I told myself over and over how lucky I was and that this must mean I really was a good violinist. But the moment I got there, I knew I'd made a terrible mistake. I liked music, but not all day and every day. Those other students wanted to eat, breathe, and sleep music, while I just wanted to be back at Alta Mesa with my friends.

"Mom, we've been through this a million times," I said quickly. "The conservatory wasn't for me. I don't think I want to be a professional violinist. That doesn't mean I want to drop the violin totally, but I do want a normal life, a life that includes more than

43

the violin." I looked up at her, willing her to understand. "You want me to be happy, don't you?"

She didn't smile. "In the old country, the parents made the decisions. They knew what was best because they were old and wise. And the children did what they were told. They respected their parents."

"So you mean to tell me that if your parents told you you'd have to work in a fish market or as a stripper, you'd just do it?"

"Parents wouldn't give such bad advice," she snapped. "They always wanted what was best for a child, the way we do. When they saw a child had a great talent, they would want her to pursue this talent, like we do now."

I sighed and took a big gulp of milk. It wasn't going to change. Since I'd quit the music conservatory, they'd been mad at me. They never came out and said they were angry or yelled. They didn't do stuff like that. But we hadn't gone through a single day without my mother mentioning the conservatory. It didn't look like they were going to forgive or forget.

I gulped down the last of my milk and got up. "I'd better get started on my homework," I said. "I have a column to write tonight."

My mother only sniffed. I picked up my book bag and went through to my bedroom. What could I do to make them understand how I felt? It wasn't that I hated the violin. I loved playing in the school orchestra. But those intense, dedicated students at the conservatory scared me. All they wanted to talk about was their music. They didn't feel that anything else mattered, and I couldn't feel that way. I wanted to have fun and date guys and go to dances and choose a career when I came out of college, not right now. And I was pretty sure that career wouldn't be standing up all alone on a stage, playing the violin.

I tipped my books out onto the bed. The first thing I did was shove the chemistry book to one side. I'd get to that later. It always took me hours to read through a chapter and try to understand what Mr. Parnow had been trying to say. *Maybe I can call Adam if I have problems,* I thought. *He seemed to understand okay. I wouldn't mind an excuse to talk to him.*

But first I was going to write my column. I was so excited that I could hardly hold my pen. My first real column for a real newspaper. This had to be good. I wanted everyone to read it and say, "Wow, that Bobby person gives great advice. What witty answers—such insight!"

I stared at the blank page in front of me. *Okay, so start writing,* I commanded myself. *Think up some good problems.*

Now that I actually had to write something, I

wasn't sure where to start. My own life—that would be a good place to get ideas. What problems did I have?

Dear Bobby: My mom tries to live my life for me. What should I do to make her understand that I'm old enough to make my own decisions?

Good question. The only problem was that I didn't know the answer. Besides, it wasn't the kind of fun, glamorous question that readers wanted. I had to sound like the daytime talk shows, only not as sexy. So what other problems had I seen around school? Being bugged by Jeremy was the obvious one.

Dear Bobby: This creepy guy keeps following me around and he won't take no for an answer. What should I do?
                    Signed: Going Crazy.

Dear Going Crazy: The easiest way to get rid of him is to find yourself another guy, fast. And preferably a two-hundred-pound linebacker. The creepy guy won't want to risk tackling him!

I smiled to myself as I wrote it. *Good answer, Karen.* If only I could find myself a linebacker . . . except I found most football players more interested in football than girls. Like Ben and Ginger. Which gave me another idea. . . .

I started writing again.

Dear Bobby: I've been going with this guy for a year now. I really like him, but he's a football player and he always puts football before me. I never see him during football season. Do you think I should dump him and find someone who can give me more time?
                    Signed: Football Widow.

Dear Football Widow: Football doesn't take up twenty-four hours of every day. If he can't find a few minutes every once in a while to call you and tell you you're special, I'd say he needs a wake-up call. I'll bet there are plenty of guys out there who would love to pay you more attention. I say go for it!

Great answer! I was on a roll now. I was lucky that right now all my friends had problems that needed solving. Roni was still hoping that Josh would lose his feelings for Ginger and stop thinking of Roni as only a friend. . . .

Dear Bobby: I'm dying to get to know this boy better, but he just thinks of me as a

friend. What can I do to change things?
                              Signed: Depressed.

Dear Depressed: I hate to say this, but all guys' minds work the same way. If you come across to him as one of the guys, then you'd better turn yourself into a superbabe. It's amazing how short skirts, sexy T-shirts, and makeup will wake up any guy. Try it and see.

I grinned to myself. I'd never suggest something like that to Roni in real life, but it was the sort of answer you'd find in magazines, wasn't it?

Which just left Justine. This was a hard one, because I couldn't see any way that Justine and Jeremy would ever get together. She was everything he didn't want in a girl. But I had to give it a try.

Dear Bobby: I like this guy who doesn't even notice I exist. We are total opposites and I can't think how to get him to notice me. Can opposites ever attract?
                              Signed: Hopeless.

Dear Hopeless: Don't give up hope. Sometimes the weirdest people wind up finding happiness together. But you have to find some common ground to get you started.

Study his lifestyle—is there anywhere you'd be likely to bump into him? The same pizza place, maybe? If not, then I'm afraid you'll just have to fake it and bone up on one of his interests. Good luck. Hope it works for you.

I sat back and admired my work. This was a great column I'd written. They'd have to be impressed when Brad read it out loud at the next staff meeting. Even Gabrielle would have to admit that I wasn't just a humble closet cleaner. I'd show her who knew something about life!

I copied my questions and answers out neatly to hand in to Brad, then I tackled my homework. I was dying to call Roni or Ginger or Justine and tell them about the column, but Brad had made me promise I wouldn't tell anyone. Did that include my best friends? I hoped not. After all, what was the point of writing a killer column if nobody knew who'd written it?

I zipped through my homework and I even understood the chemistry for once, so I didn't have an excuse to call Adam. At least I could show him the column. He knew who Dear Bobby was. I grinned to myself as I imagined how impressed he'd be. If only he'd get himself a column, too, we could work on them together . . . just what I was saying in the column about common ground and shared interests.

I stopped and thought about this. I'd never had a boyfriend who shared my interests before. Okay, so I'd only had one real boyfriend in my life, and James was certainly his own person with his own interests. He'd tried being supportive, but it hadn't worked. He was so wrapped up in his computers that I just messed up his lifestyle. He'd been a great first boyfriend, but now I wanted someone I could have fun with. And I had a feeling that Adam might be the right kind of guy. Our minds were totally on the same wavelength, weren't they? I'd picked up on his pantomime this morning right away. And we were both shy and he was so sweet and thoughtful. *Yeah,* I decided. *I could do worse.* The newspaper was turning out to be just great for me.

I couldn't wait to get to school the next morning and hand in that column to Brad. I bugged my mother to hurry up while she cut my sandwiches into annoyingly perfect triangles.

"What's the big rush?" she demanded.

"I want to get to school early so that I can hand in my first column to the editor."

"Hmmmph," she said as she stuffed the sandwich into my lunch bag and thrust it at me. "Go ahead, ignore your violin. Ignore your talent. Write this newspaper column, if that's what you think will make you happy. But I tell you you'll be sorry. In a year's time you'll come back to me and say you want to apply to the conservatory again. You'll come to your senses. You'll see."

"Oh, Mom." I sighed. "Won't you ever give up?"

"Not until you're back where you belong," she said.

I snatched up my book bag and stomped out of the house. *Dear Bobby,* I muttered to myself. *I need to find a way to get rid of my mother in a hurry. Any suggestions?*

Chapter

5

"Hey, Karen, wait up," Roni called as I ran down the hall. "What's the big hurry?"

"Oh, hi, Roni. I've just got to drop this off at the newspaper office before school. I was hoping to catch Brad there so that I could give it to him personally."

Roni's eyes lit up. "So they gave you a real writing assignment this year? No more cleaning closets?"

"No more closets." I sighed happily. "I've got my own column."

"You have? What's it about?"

"It's . . ." I suddenly remembered I wasn't supposed to tell. "Just a general sort of column. Sort of funny and serious at the same time."

"That's great, Karen. Will your name be at the top of it?"

"I don't think so."

"You should get your name on your column. Go to that editor and insist!" Roni said. "Demand your rights. We'll come with you if you like and tell him that you're fantastic."

I laughed. "Thanks, but everything's okay, really."

See, I knew this would turn out to be hard. I'd have to tell them, but they wouldn't blab. We'd kept each other's secrets before. "I have to run, Roni. See you second period, right?"

"Okay. And let me know if you bump into Justine. She just ran past me and was acting very odd. She was in a hurry and wouldn't say where she was going. . . ."

"Maybe she's going to the nerd hall to hide in Jeremy's locker and lie in wait for him," I suggested. "Wouldn't that be great?"

"Only she wasn't heading that way," Roni said. "I hope she hasn't come up with another crazy idea."

"You know Justine," I said. "See ya, Roni. I'll keep an eye out for her."

I waved, then sprinted up the stairs to the newspaper office. As I'd hoped, Brad was there. He looked up when I came in.

"Hi, Karen. What's up?"

"I've got my first column for you," I said, and held it out to him.

"That was quick. You don't waste any time, do you?" he said. "Just put it there on my desk, will you? I'll take a look at it later."

I wanted to tell him that he had to look at it right now and tell me how good it was, but he was frowning at a column of figures. "I'm trying to see how we can keep within our budget," he said. "The cost of paper has doubled. I'm meeting with the faculty adviser at lunchtime today. I just hope he doesn't insist that we cut back to four pages."

My heart lurched. If we cut back, my column would be the first thing to go. And I was so close to success! I found I was holding my breath as I headed for the music room and first-period orchestra class.

Usually I really enjoyed orchestra. It was a great feeling to be part of a big group, making music. The standard was very high and we sounded great together. We played a lot of fun music, too, not just old classical stuff but modern pop songs rewritten for orchestra. Right now we were doing a Beatles medley and music from the *Phantom of the Opera*.

I was still worrying about losing my column as I came into the music room. I walked right past the woodwind section, hoping that Jeremy hadn't seen me.

"Hi, Karen!" Jeremy's voice chimed; he had

found me. He must have been taking lessons from Owen, because his voice was about one inch from my ear. I jumped a mile.

"Oh, Jeremy, you scared me. I didn't see you."

"I just wanted to tell you," he said, "that I'm working on a full orchestration of that song I wrote for you at camp. I'm going to ask Mr. Healey if we can perform it when it's done. Did you ever imagine you'd have an entire orchestra playing a love song for you, Karen?"

"Not in my wildest dreams," I said, thinking, *Only in my worst nightmares!*

He smiled. "You must know how serious I am about you. I'm pouring my soul into this piece."

Oh, help, I thought as I took my place. I was trapped for life. Nothing I could do would ever get rid of Jeremy. *Dear Bobby: What am I going to do now, apart from join the foreign legion?*

I glanced at my watch. It was already ten after eight.

"Where's Mr. Healey?" I asked Amy Schwarz, who sat beside me.

"He went into the instrument room with some girl," she said. "He's been in there quite a while."

I started getting my music in order and tuned my violin so that I was all ready to start. I could hear restless sounds around me. Rich Baker, one of the senior trumpeters, got up. "Maybe we should start warm-ups until Mr. Healey gets here," he suggested.

We had just picked up our instruments when Mr. Healey appeared from the back room. Someone was following him, carrying a marching-band tuba.

"So see how it goes and maybe you'll be ready to march with us next week," he said. "It's really simple music once you get the breathing right."

As the person with the tuba staggered past me, my jaw dropped. "What are you . . ."

"Guess what, Karen," Justine squealed excitedly. "I'm going to take up the tuba!"

My mouth was still hanging wide open. Justine giggled. "Don't look so surprised. I went and asked Mr. Healey what instrument I should take up and he said we didn't have a single tuba for the marching band this year, so I volunteered. He's even loaned me the tuba. Isn't that wonderful?"

I couldn't believe it. Justine was willing to lug a huge tuba around the football field, making a fool of herself, just for Jeremy? As silly as it seemed, I knew that she was determined to win Jeremy's heart, and I'd never be able to talk her out of this one.

"Justine, the tuba's a very big instrument. I've never seen a girl march with one before. You really think you'll be able to blow notes from it?"

"Sure," she said. "I'm in top physical shape,

remember. I was the star tennis player last spring, so I have to have good lungs, don't I? And I plan to find myself the best tuba teacher in the country, even if I have to fly him in from New York. I'll take lessons every night, and I should be oom-pahing away just fine in a week." She leaned close to me. "And *you-know-who* will have to be impressed at that, right? Only girl tuba player in the state of Arizona. That's pretty hot stuff."

Then she picked up the huge instrument again. "My only problem," she added as she staggered to the door, "is carrying this thing. It weighs a ton. Do you think I could hire someone to carry it for me when we march?"

She didn't wait for an answer, and I was still staring at the door long after she had gone. I couldn't believe that Justine could learn the tuba in a week. Actually, I couldn't imagine her getting a single note out of it! But Justine did do amazing things when she was determined. And she probably would fly in the world's top tuba player, too. She had the money to do crazy things like that. I just hoped Jeremy would be as impressed as she thought he'd be.

"Have you written your first column yet?" Adam asked as soon as I came into the chemistry lab.

I nodded. "Would you like to take a look? I kept a copy for myself."

His face lit up the way I had hoped Brad's would. "Sure, I'd love to. Thanks."

I handed it to him and held my breath while he read it. I saw him smile a couple of times, then he looked up. "This is good stuff, Karen. Boy, you weren't kidding about knowing how to solve your friends' problems. These are great answers, and funny, too. It should be an instant hit!"

"You think so?" I asked excitedly, until I remembered. "There's just one small problem," I added. "Brad says that the newspaper is going over budget and he's got to find ways to cut corners. I bet this column is the first to go."

"No way," Adam said angrily. "I'll tell him that he'd be out of his mind to cancel this. Get rid of Steve and his stupid sports first!"

I laughed. "I can see that happening, can't you? Most kids only read the paper for the sports. But it's nice of you to want to speak up for me. I just wish you'd do it more for yourself."

"Ah," he said. "Well, that's harder. I'm able to forget that I'm shy when I feel strongly enough about someone else."

What had he meant by that? Was he saying that he felt strongly about me? I gave him a quick sideways glance, but he was still staring at my column.

"I mean, I hate to see other people walked over, because I know what it feels like," he added.

I took my place across from him. "So did you ask Brad for an assignment?"

He nodded. "He said he wasn't sure yet. He thought he might need a faculty reporter to keep tabs on what was going on with the teachers."

It sounded boring to me. "Would you want to do that?"

"It's a job, isn't it? Better than cleaning closets. And anyway, I'm more comfortable talking to teachers than other kids. Teachers don't laugh when you make a fool of yourself."

"I'm going to have to find a way to give you a big confidence boost, Adam Bateman," I said. "You're smart. You're funny. You shouldn't worry about what other people think."

"But I do," he said. "I can't help it. I'm terrified of saying the wrong thing."

I nodded. "I know how you feel," I said, "because I feel the same way. I guess some people are just born shy and there's nothing we can do about it."

"Except stick together and speak up for each other," he said. Then he gave me a shy smile. He had a very nice smile.

We had good news at our next newspaper staff meeting. Brad had managed to get our budget raised, so my column didn't have to be cut.

"Karen's turned in a fine first column," Brad announced. "I'm really looking forward to seeing what kind of questions we get once it comes out."

"Dear Bobby: I really like this cool babe, but she keeps turning me down when I ask her for a date—what should I do?" Steve clowned in a wimpy voice. "Dear Wimpy: Try caveman tactics. Hit her over the head and drag her off," he finished with a grin at Gabrielle. "You reckon it would work, Gaby?"

"In your dreams," Gabrielle said crushingly. "And my name is Gabrielle." She turned to her friends. "Whatever happened to romantic men? They just don't exist anymore. Only boring jocks fill these hallways."

"Okay, people, back to work," Brad said quickly. "Gabrielle, what do we have for the lead story?"

Gabrielle tossed all those incredible blond curls. "We're just completing our survey on cheating. I think we've got enough good stuff to make a lead story out of that. Did you know that over sixty percent of the student body admits to cheating when they get the chance?"

"Well, I certainly do." Steve laughed.

Brad smiled. "There you are, Gabrielle. First-person quote."

"So you think that will work as a lead story, then?" she asked.

"Sounds great to me," Brad said. "Oh, and before I forget. I've told Adam that I want him to be our faculty-news person, so save a corner for a 'what the teachers are doing this week' column, okay?"

Gabrielle looked at Adam as if she were being told to save a corner for a cockroach. "If you say so," she said flatly. "You're the boss, but I hardly think our readers are going to be interested in what the teachers are doing."

"Unless it's the X-rated stuff . . . what the girls PE teacher is doing with the football coach behind the bleachers," Steve said.

"Shut up, Steve. You are so gross!" Gabrielle snapped in Steve's direction. "Even if there was stuff like that going on, *he'd* never be able to find it out."

And *she'd* never win the Miss Congeniality award, I decided. If you weren't a cute senior guy, forget it. As far as Gabrielle was concerned, you didn't exist.

"I hope you can dig up a real scandal among the teachers," I muttered to Adam as we left the newspaper office. "I'd love to see Gabrielle's face."

"So would I," he agreed.

"I'll put my friends into action spying for you," I said. "They're great at finding out things. They've been bugging me about the column I'm writing. I told them I wasn't supposed to tell, but they said they'd know as soon as the paper comes out anyway. I'm sure they will. I used their problems. . . ."

Adam looked at me and then laughed nervously. "You used your friends' real problems? Are you sure that was smart? Won't they be mad at you?"

"Because I used their problems in my column? I don't see why. I didn't identify them by name, and I had to come up with made-up problems in a hurry. Where else was I going to look?"

"I guess you know what you're doing," Adam said. "But I'm not sure I'd want my problems splashed across a newspaper. It would be like seeing yourself in the supermarket tabloids."

I laughed. "Give me a break, Adam. They were very ordinary problems and very lame answers. I didn't say that one of them was dating a Martian or was a reincarnation of Cleopatra . . . although come to think of it . . ."

Adam laughed, too. "There you are. You've got your next column all thought out."

We reached the front door and went down the steps.

"Bye, Karen, see you tomorrow," Adam said.

"Bye, Adam."

He went one way and I went the other. I'd sort of hoped he would walk home with me. We seemed to be getting along so well. I had to remind myself that he was even shyer than I was. He'd have to be very sure that I liked him, too before he showed any interest in me, because his ego couldn't take being rejected.

I didn't care. Right now I was enjoying being just friends.

When I got home, my mother was waiting in the kitchen as usual.

"So Karen, why are you late?" she asked.

"I told you, Mom. I had a newspaper meeting after school," I said.

"You're sure it was a meeting? You weren't meeting some boy and not telling us about it?"

"Oh, Mom, please." I sighed. "Do we have to start all that again?" She had given me the hardest time when I was dating James.

"So you're telling me that you don't have a boyfriend right now? There is no boy in your life?"

I sank onto the stool and looked longingly at the chocolate chip cookies. "No, Mom. There's no boy in my life. I haven't had a boyfriend since James, remember?"

She looked pleased. "That's good to hear. I don't want my daughter sneaking around behind my back. But you are fifteen years old now. Maybe your daddy and I have been too strict with you."

There was something weird about the way she was looking at me.

"So what are you saying?" I asked cautiously.

"What I'm saying is this. If you want to date a suitable boy, a boy your father and I approve of, then we wouldn't say no. You'd have our blessing."

She was smiling to herself as if she knew something that I didn't. I got the feeling that my mother was up to something.

Chapter

6

On Monday morning the first edition of the *Alta Mesa Heights* came out. All the way to school I felt exactly the way I used to feel before a violin recital. My heart was thumping and my palms were sweaty. I just hoped everyone liked it. I guess I dreamed of walking around campus and hearing people saying, "You have to read that Dear Bobby column. It's so good. I wonder who wrote it?"

Then I got scared that other people would find it so blah that they wouldn't even read it.

As it turned out, I was wrong on both counts. My friends noticed it right away. They were waiting for me under the tree as I came out at lunch. And they didn't look too happy.

"Nice column, Karen," Ginger said, waving the paper at me.

"Uh . . . thanks," I said timidly. She didn't exactly sound thrilled.

"Yeah, Karen, it didn't take too many brains to figure out which column was yours," Roni said.

"I didn't figure it out right away, I have to admit," Justine said. "But when Roni and Ginger pointed out to me that all the problems were just like ours, I felt the same way they did. I didn't know you could be so mean, Karen."

"I wasn't being mean!" My cheeks were burning hot now.

"Oh, come on, Karen. Those were our problems in the newspaper for everyone to read," Ginger said.

"I had to make up my own questions and answers for the first column," I said. "I couldn't invent problems out of thin air. . . ."

"So you chose ours," Roni said.

I looked from one angry face to the next. "Look, guys, it's not as if anyone else will read the paper and know who you are. . . ."

"Oh, no?" Ginger said. "My boyfriend puts football ahead of me? Ben's not stupid, you know. He'll think I've been writing to the newspaper."

"Ginger, Ben's not the only football player with a girlfriend, you know. And even if Ben does think you wrote it, isn't that what you wanted?" I asked. "Your problem will be out in the open, and maybe Ben will change and try to be more attentive."

"And maybe he'll think I don't want him anymore and he'll start looking at other girls."

"The point is, Karen," Roni said coldly, "that we didn't give you permission to write about our problems. Our worries are, well, personal. We told you because you're our friend—or we thought you were our friend. We didn't expect you to go blabbing all over the school, and we especially didn't expect you to give us cutesy answers."

"Yeah, Karen," Justine said. "Telling Roni to wear short skirts and sexy T-shirts to get Josh's attention—that was so tacky. You know she's not that kind of person. She doesn't even have the legs for short skirts like I do."

"It wasn't meant to be advice for Roni," I said hastily, because she was glaring at Justine now. "It was just the sort of witty answer they give in newspaper columns."

"And what if someone writes to you for real advice and you give a dumb answer, like that stuff about dating a two-hundred-pound linebacker?" Ginger demanded. "There might be kids with real problems who really want help. You could do serious damage to people's lives."

"I'd be more careful of what I said if it was a real problem," I said quickly.

"Gee, thanks a lot, Karen," Justine snapped. "You'd be more careful with strangers, but you can say what you like about us, huh?"

"I didn't mean it that way." I looked around desperately. For once I'd even have welcomed an invasion of the nerds. Owen's repulsive grin two inches from my face would have been better than seeing my friends glaring at me. "Look, you guys," I began cautiously. "I'm sorry I upset you. I didn't think you'd mind if I used your problems, because I was sure nobody else would know I was talking about you. You know I'd never blab about any real secret you told me. Those things I wrote were so general that they'd apply to most people. I really didn't think I was letting you down." I looked at them hopefully. "Please say you forgive me. I promise I'll never write about your problems in public again."

"At least the advice you gave me was actually quite good," Justine added. "You told me to take up some of his interests and I'm learning the tuba. Or at least I will be learning the tuba when I can find a teacher. Do you know that there are no tuba teachers in the yellow pages? I've had to put a call in to the Boston Pops. So far I just blow and nothing comes out."

"I just hope you haven't totally *blown* it for me

and Ben." Ginger pushed her hair back from her face.

"But you said you were thinking of finding someone else," I reminded her.

"And if I do decide to do that, he'll think it's because I took the advice in some dumb column."

"Look, I've said I was sorry. Do you want me to print an apology? 'Dear Readers: I apologize for printing Ginger, Roni, and Justine's problems for all the world to read about.'"

"Don't you dare," three voices said at the same time. Their laughter broke some of the tension, but I felt terrible all afternoon, even as I headed to the newspaper office after school.

Adam joined me halfway up the stairs. "Hi, Karen. How's the star columnist?"

"Not feeling much like a star."

He looked at me with those solemn dark eyes. "What's up?" he asked.

"You were right. My friends are all mad at me for using their problems in my column. I didn't think they'd be upset, because nobody could possibly know it was them, but they are." I gave a big sigh. "I hate having people mad at me. Now I'm mad at myself for hurting my friends."

He smiled. "You're just discovering the price of fame. You can't please all of the people all of the time."

"It looks like I've ended up pleasing all of the people *none* of the time."

"You're wrong there," he said. "I've heard some good things about your column today. A group of seniors sitting at the table next to mine in the cafeteria were trying to figure out who Dear Bobby was. They thought you gave great answers. One of them said it was probably an English teacher who wrote it."

"No kidding?" I actually smiled.

"And for what it's worth, I thought it was really good too," he said.

"Thanks, Adam. But I can tell you, the next column I write is going to be different. No more smart answers that I don't really mean. I'm going to be very careful about what I say when I get genuine questions, because Ginger's right."

"What did she say?"

"She said that my answers could affect people's lives. When I get some real questions, I'm going to think through my answers very carefully. I didn't realize it before, but this column really gives me a chance to help people with their problems." I glanced up at him. "I just hope I can do it."

He smiled reassuringly. "You can do it."

We reached the office door. The loud buzz of conversation from inside showed that we were some of the last few to arrive.

"I hope somebody actually writes in for the next issue," I said. "I've already used up my friends' problems. I don't know if I'm creative enough to come up with any more."

"I'm sure you'll get tons of mail," Adam said. He stood aside to let me go into the newspaper office first. *Such a gentleman,* I thought, *and so nice.* He'd tried to say the right things to make me feel better. I found myself thinking about what my mother had said. She wouldn't mind my having a boyfriend if he was the sort of boy she approved of. I snuck a quick look at Adam. There wasn't anything about him to disapprove of, was there?

Adam was pretending to concentrate hard on the newspaper in front of him. That's when I realized that I hadn't even bothered to look for his column. I'd been gloating over mine, then worrying about mine, and I hadn't said one word about his.

Hastily I turned the pages, and there it was, at the bottom of page two. *Teacher Talk,* by Adam Bateman. I began to read.

There is no truth to the rumor that Mr. Fisher's new hairstyle is a toupee. The fact that Mr. Fisher stood watching the entire football game last Friday in a howling gale and his hair stayed put proves that it has to be real. I found my lips twitching into a smile. *Principal Lazarow climbed Mount McKinley during his trip to Alaska this summer. He has the photo of himself standing on the summit proudly displayed in his office. At least, the picture shows a lot of blue sky behind and snow around his feet, so we have to believe that he's just climbed a mountain, right?*

My smile broadened as I read on. Adam had managed to take boring, ordinary facts and make them amusing. He wrote very well, way better than I did. In fact, he had an absolute flair.

I nudged him. "This is really good," I said, pointing to his column.

He shrugged, turning pink with embarrassment. "I don't think anyone else has even noticed it yet."

"Then they should. You must be one of the best writers they've got. I think they should give you a bigger assignment—a lead news piece or an editorial commentary. Do you want me to suggest it to Brad for you?"

He shook his head firmly. "I'm okay. Actually, I enjoy interviewing teachers. And I get my name on my writing this way. So thanks for the offer, but I'm fine, Karen. I've got almost three more years to make a name for myself." His eyes met mine. "Who knows? Maybe we'll be co-editors by the time we're seniors. And then go to journalism school at Columbia together, and then both work for the *Washington Post*. . . ."

"Whoa, wait a second." I laughed. "I don't even

74

know if writing is what I want to do. I'm just trying to persuade my parents to stop planning out one career for me, and now you've started doing the same thing."

"Sorry," he said. "But I've always known what I want to do. And you write so well, I thought you could do it with me. It would be fun to do things with a friend."

"Yeah, I guess it would," I said. I realized that I'd never had a guy for a friend before. I wondered if he ever thought of moving beyond friends. What would happen if we did?

Adam wasn't actually right about Dear Bobby getting tons of mail. All week long nothing showed up in my pigeonhole at the newspaper. The deadline for the next issue was getting closer and I really didn't want to invent phony problems again. I didn't think I could come up anything that didn't sound dumb or childish.

Finally on Friday, Brad called to me as I was on my way to orchestra. "There's a letter for Dear Bobby in the office. I thought you'd like to know."

"Thanks," I called. I changed direction and sprinted up the stairs. There it was in my pigeonhole. A real letter addressed to Dear Bobby in small, neat writing. I ripped it open.

Dear Bobby: I need help badly. I'm in love with this girl, but she doesn't even know I exist. I just can't stop thinking about her, but I can't seem to come up with a way to tell her how I feel. What can I do to win her affection? I know I have to tread carefully so that I don't blow my chances with her. She's very special. Thanks in advance for your help.

Signed: Hopeful.

"Guess what," I whispered to Adam as I passed him in the chemistry lab. "I just got my first real Dear Bobby letter. I'll show it to you." I put it in front of him. "It's great, huh? Just the sort of thing we need for the column. I'm going to try and think up an answer during chemistry. Nudge me if Mr. Parnow is looking in my direction."

"Okay," Adam said, and handed the letter back to me.

I slipped it between the pages of my chemistry book and chewed on my pen while I tried to come up with the right answer. I just wished I knew more about the person who had written the letter. It was hard to write an answer without knowing more. The guy might be a complete nerd. It might even be Jeremy, trying to find a way to get together with me. I shuddered at the thought. I certainly wouldn't want to risk encouraging him.

*Dear Hopeful: Try moving to Alaska and for-
get about her. . . .*

But what if it wasn't Jeremy? What if it was some
nice guy whose heart was breaking right now?
Keep it light, I decided. Don't get too serious. If
you make him too hopeful, he'll be hurt if she turns
him down.

Dear Hopeful, I wrote.

> *First of all, you have to do something to
> make her notice you. You say she doesn't even
> know you exist. Sounds to me as if you might
> just be too shy or quiet or ordinary right now.*

I chewed on my pen again, trying to think of
what would make me notice a guy. I remembered
Damien, but he was always a total extrovert. You
couldn't help noticing him. He didn't mind being in
the limelight. But then there was James. He'd been
kind of shy and yet he'd given me a red rose once,
right there in the hallway where everybody could
see. That was very sweet. I started writing again.

> *You're going to have to take chances to
> make her notice you. In fact, you might have
> to do something pretty spectacular. Find out*

what would impress her and then do it. No
girl can resist a romantic hero.

When Mr. Parnow wasn't looking, I scribbled,
What do you think? and passed it across to Adam.

I saw his cheeks turn pink as he read it, but he
nodded solemnly and passed it back. Then he made
an "okay" sign.

At the end of class he stood beside me as I put
my binder into my book bag. "Uh, Karen, I've been
thinking," he said. "Do you have to go straight
home after school tonight?"

"No, not right away."

"I just wondered," he said. "Maybe we could go
for coffee or ice cream. I'd really like to talk to you,
somewhere away from this place, and I just wondered . . ." He wasn't looking at me. He was staring
down at his shoe.

"I'd love to," I said brightly.

He looked up then. "You would? That's great,
Karen. I'll wait for you outside the front gate then,
okay?"

"Fine."

"See you then."

"Okay. See you."

I hurried down the hall. Adam had asked me
out—well, not exactly on a date, but it was a good
start. We'd sit together eating ice cream or drinking

coffee and we'd get to know each other better. As I turned the corner, heading for my locker, all thoughts of Adam were suddenly sucked from my mind. Jeremy was standing at the end of the hall, waiting for me again! I just prayed that things went well with Adam this afternoon. Pretty soon I might have a boyfriend and Jeremy would see us walking around school holding hands and he'd finally get the message.

I slowly continued toward my locker, focusing on what I'd say to Jeremy *this* time to make him leave.

Chapter

7

I walked cautiously down the path in the direction of our tree. I could see Roni already attacking a giant sandwich. She always stays so skinny, no matter what she eats! Justine was opening one of those clear plastic boxes from the deli. Probably some exotic salad again. Yesterday it had been watermelon and feta cheese. Ginger must have just arrived, too, because she was unzipping her backpack. She looked up and saw me.

"Hi, Karen," she called.

I swallowed hard. "Hi," I said, and sat down. Although they seemed to be acting normal, I got the feeling that I wasn't so welcome anymore. They were still mad at me for writing about their problems. Nothing had happened because of it—Ben hadn't broken up with Ginger and nobody had guessed their identities—but I could still feel a distance between us, and I hated it.

"So let's talk about tomorrow," Roni said, waving her sandwich around. "Whose turn is it?"

She was talking about our Saturday night sleepovers. We usually took turns hosting them. I was just thinking that it was probably my turn when Justine said, "I don't care whose turn it is. I want you to come over to my place. I'm going to be taking my first tuba lesson tomorrow morning. I have to show you what I've learned and I'm not dragging that tuba around to anyone else's house."

"How did you find a tuba teacher in the end?" Ginger asked. "Are you flying in the Boston Pops tuba player for the day?"

Justine grinned. "No, silly. Christine called the conservatory and they have a guy there who gives private lessons. Just think, Karen. I'll be going to the conservatory where you almost went. I'll be walking in and out with real musicians. If only we could arrange to have Jeremy go past, just as I'm coming out . . ."

"Staggering with her tuba," Roni finished.

"He'd never recognize you with that tuba wrapped around you anyway," Ginger added.

Justine glared at us. "You guys don't believe this will work, do you? You don't think I'll be able to learn the tuba. Well, you'll be surprised. I'm going to practice like crazy and in a couple of weeks there I'll be, marching with the band—the only girl tuba player in the state. You can get your newspaper to do a feature on me, Karen."

"I wouldn't let Karen do it. She'd probably mention that you're only doing this to impress Jeremy," Ginger said.

"Hey, that's not fair," I snapped. "So I did something dumb, but I never meant to upset you . . . and nothing bad happened because of it. So give me a break and forget it, please. Because if you don't, I'm going to eat lunch somewhere else." I readied myself to stand up and leave, if need be.

"She's right," Roni said. "We're acting like it was a big deal when it wasn't. And she didn't mean any harm. Sit down, Karen. We won't mention it again, okay? We'll pretend it never happened."

"So let's get back to my tuba," Justine said. "If you all come over to my place, I'll play something for you. I wonder if anyone wrote concertos for the tuba. Karen?"

"I think you're being a little optimistic there, Justine," I said. "I don't imagine the tuba is easy to play. It might take weeks before you can get a note out of it."

"For you, maybe," Justine said, "because you don't have my lung power. But don't forget that I went to school on top of a mountain. I've seen *National Geographic*. People who live that high up develop fantastic heart and lungs as a result of all that mountain air. I'll be blowing 'Mary Had a Little Lamb' before you know it."

Roni glanced at me and winked, which made me feel better.

"Guess what," I said. "I just got a real Dear Bobby letter. I'm going to show it to you guys tomorrow night. We can talk about it and you can check out the answer I've written and see if it's okay. I don't want to risk goofing again."

"Hey, that's cool. We all get to be Dear Bobby," Roni said. "I wonder what kind of person would really write to Dear Bobby. Does the guy sound like a weirdo, Karen?"

Justine tossed back her hair. "Either it's a joke or he's a total loser," she said. "Normal, healthy people like us would never need to take their problems to a newspaper. They'd just go to their own shrink."

We all burst out laughing. "Justine, you're too much," Ginger said.

"Why? What have I said?" Justine looked offended.

"Your own shrink? Who has their own shrink?" Ginger demanded.

"Everyone in my neighborhood has their own

psychiatrist," Justine said breezily. "At least by the time they're in high school."

"I've got my own shrink," Roni said. "She's called Ginger, and sometimes Karen and sometimes Justine."

"Maybe the person who writes to Dear Bobby doesn't have friends," I said. "Or maybe he's scared his friends would laugh at him."

"Then they're not true friends," Ginger said.

"You just laughed at me," Justine said indignantly.

"That's different." Ginger grinned. "You say funny things."

"I do not. I say very natural, intelligent things and you always laugh," Justine said. "If I wasn't so well balanced, I'd get a terrible inferiority complex and have to see a shrink about it."

Roni turned to her. "Here, have an oatmeal raisin cookie, Justine. We all love you, even if you are weird."

We ate for a while in silence and then I remembered my other news. "And I might have something else to tell you guys tomorrow," I said. "You know that tall boy with the curly hair who works on the newspaper with me?"

"Adam? The one you told us about?" Ginger asked.

I nodded. "He asked me out for coffee or ice

cream after school. I think he likes me, but he's kind of shy."

"Hey, Karen! New school year, new guy," Roni said, giving me a high five.

"And if Karen finds herself a new boyfriend, then Jeremy will stop chasing her and I can chase him instead," Justine said. "Jeremy and my tuba and I can live happily ever after."

"Do you like him, Karen?" Ginger asked.

"I think so," I said. "He's my type—you know, quiet, sensitive but with a good sense of humor. We get along just great at the newspaper meetings."

"Then go for it, girl," Ginger said.

I remembered Ginger's encouragement as I hurried out of school to meet Adam. Coming down the steps, I thought I saw a figure standing in the deep shade between the bushes. Maybe I was getting paranoid, but it looked a lot like Jeremy. This was my big chance to let him know that he was wasting his time.

"Adam!" I yelled, and ran across the school yard. His face broke into a big smile when he saw me.

"Hi, Karen, thanks for coming," he said. "Where would you like to go?"

"There's an Italian ice-cream place on Central," I suggested. "I've never been in there, but I like Italian ice cream."

"Sounds good to me," Adam said. "We'll need ice cream by the time we get there."

We walked along the hot, dusty sidewalk. Heat rose up from the asphalt. I pushed my sticky bangs back from my face. Great, so I'd look disgusting by the time we got there. It wasn't possible to go anywhere in Phoenix without sweating unless you had an air-conditioned car.

"Gee, it's hot," Adam said. "I don't usually walk this far."

"How do you get around?"

He blushed. "My mom picks me up. She has to get my little sister anyway, so she swings by to get me."

"Lucky you. We only have one car and my dad needs it, so I have to walk everywhere or take the bus."

"My mom babies me," he said. "She does everything for me. I think that's why I've never learned to fight my own battles."

"You'd better put your foot down soon," I said. "Or she'll want to come to college with you."

He laughed. "You better believe it. I'm going to look at schools in New England. Anywhere that's too far to visit each weekend. Although I will miss her doing my laundry."

"Adam!" I laughed. I was about to give him a friendly push, but then I remembered how shy he

87

was and pulled back my hand at the last second.

I was really glad when we reached the ice-cream parlor. Adam ordered a hot fudge sundae and I got a banana split. It was deliciously cool inside and we found a private table for two at the back, away from the window.

"It was really nice of you to give up your time like this, Karen," he said as soon as we were seated.

"Adam! Why wouldn't I want to spend time with you? I like talking to you."

"I feel the same way," he said. "I find it really easy to talk to you. That's why I asked you here."

I felt that something momentous was about to happen. It was like time was standing still and the rest of the world ceased to exist. Was he about to ask me out on a real date?

"You seem to be so wise," he went on. "You know about things. I knew you had to be the right person. Today I was sure of it."

He looked at me and I gave him my most encouraging smile.

"I think you should know," he said slowly, "that I wrote that letter to Dear Bobby."

"You did? Why didn't you say so sooner?"

"For the same reason that I wrote the letter. Whenever I try to tell someone how I feel, I clam up—I just can't seem to get the right words out when it really matters. Somehow I find it easier to put my thoughts down on paper."

"But Adam, you know me well enough by now," I said. "You can come right out and tell me what you feel."

"Oh, I'm sure you'll understand and you won't laugh at me or anything," he said softly.

"You know I'd never do that."

"But this is so important to me. If I don't find the right words, I'll blow it forever."

"Adam, you won't blow it forever. For pete's sake, have more confidence in yourself! Why would you blow it if you don't find the right words?"

"Because it would be my only chance with her. I know that much."

I didn't think I was hearing right. "Excuse me—with who?"

"With Gabrielle," he said. "She's the one I wrote to you about."

"Gabrielle?" I shrieked. "You brought me here to talk about Gabrielle?"

Adam turned bright red and looked around anxiously. "Shhh. Don't yell it all over the place. Someone who knows her might hear and then she'll hear about it and I'll be doomed."

I was staring at him as if he'd just turned into a three-headed Martian. He looked just the same as ever—that fresh, boyish face and those kind brown eyes and the curls that flopped over his forehead.

But he was telling me he was in love with Gabrielle!

"Let me get this straight," I stammered. "You're saying that you have a crush on Gabrielle?"

I was about to ask how he could possibly, ever in a million years, like such a snobby, stuck-up, conceited person, but he babbled right on. "I'm just crazy about her, Karen. I have to find a way to make her notice me or I'll die. You've got to help me, please. I'll do anything, anything that it takes, only please help me come up with a way to make her like me."

If I had been thinking rationally, I would have told him that he hadn't a hope in the world. There was no way that a hotshot like Gabrielle would ever look at a nobody like him. But I wasn't thinking rationally. I couldn't make my brain work at all. I heard myself saying, "Okay, I'll do what I can, Adam."

He gave me his most wonderful smile. "Thanks, Karen. You're a pal."

He was lucky I'd finished my ice cream or he might have gotten it all over his head.

Chapter

8

Surprisingly, I kept my cool all the way home. I was proud of myself. But I was still in a state of shock when I went over to Justine's house the next evening. By the time I arrived, all the others were already out by the pool, lying on lounge chairs in the shade of the big palm trees.

"Karen, over here!" Justine waved to me. "You're lucky. We saved you some punch."

"Finally you're here," Roni called as I stepped out of the shorts and T-shirt I'd been wearing over my bathing suit. "We've been dying to find out how your date with what's-his-face went. We expected you to call us last night with all the details. So what happened? Did he find the courage to ask you to go out with him?"

"Not even close," I said. "Boy, did I misread him! I guess I'm just stupid where guys are concerned."

"Why? What did he ask you out for?" Ginger asked suspiciously. "He didn't try anything, did he?"

I perched on the edge of Roni's lounger. "It turns out he wasn't interested in me at all. It was Dear Bobby he wanted."

"What?"

"He wanted me to help him get together with the girl of his dreams."

"What nerve," Roni said.

"It gets worse," I continued. "It turns out the girl of his dreams is Gabrielle Webster."

"Gabrielle?" Ginger said. "Is that the blond junior who looks like a Barbie doll?"

Roni nodded. "I've only seen her around school, but she seems like a total snob."

I agreed. "She thinks she's Miss Wonderful and she's only interested in cute senior guys. She flirted with Damien all last year."

"So your friend Adam doesn't have much of a chance with her?" Ginger asked.

"Not a prayer," I said. "She's only talked to him once that I can think of, and even then she looked at him like he was a cockroach."

"Here, drink this, you'll feel better," Justine said, pouring me a tall glass of fruit punch.

I took it and drank deeply. "I just don't get it," I said. "I just don't understand boys. I was getting along great with Adam, or so I thought. We talk together, we laugh together. I really thought he liked me. How can he possibly be interested in a snobby, rude person like Gabrielle?"

"Who can understand how guys' minds work?" Ginger said. "Certainly not the same way as ours."

"I know why he's interested in Gabrielle," I said. "She's way prettier than I am and she dresses better and she's got great hair. But I didn't think Adam cared about those things. I thought he was smarter than that."

"There are other fish in the sea, Karen," Roni said. "I'm sure there are guys out there who don't go gaga over big blue eyes and a lot of blond hair."

"Yeah, I say good riddance to him, Karen," Ginger said. "Now he's blown it with you and lost your friendship and that's his tough luck."

"Not exactly," I said.

They all looked up at me. "What are you saying?" Roni asked cautiously.

"I promised I'd help him get together with Gabrielle."

"You did what?" Roni shrieked.

"Karen, are you out of your mind? After he insulted you like that?" Justine said.

I spread my hands helplessly. "I was so shocked,

I couldn't even think straight. I heard myself saying that I'd help him."

"Let me get this straight," Ginger said. "Adam is that sort of nerdy-looking guy who's in your chemistry class?" I held up my hand to protest, but she went on, "Okay, maybe not nerdy, but definitely not one of the world's greatest hunks, right?"

I nodded.

"And Gabrielle is a junior spoiled princess who looks like a Brush-'n'-Style Barbie and you've agreed to help him get together with her?"

I sighed. "I know. I was out of my mind. But I've said I'll do it. I can't back down now. He's counting on me."

"But you just said he doesn't have a prayer," Roni reminded me.

"I know. He doesn't. What am I going to do, guys? There's no way in a million years that Gabrielle would ever go on a date with him."

"You could try secretly paying her," Justine suggested. "That sometimes works, if she's hard up for cash."

"Not that hard up," I said. "She drives a new sports car."

"I know, then," Justine went on excitedly. "We find out some terrible secret about her and we threaten to tell it to the whole school if she doesn't go on a date with Adam."

"That's called blackmail, Justine," Roni said.

"I know, but it works sometimes."

"I'm not paying and I'm not blackmailing, Justine," I said. "If I can come up with any ideas to help him, I will. I think he sees me as some kind of miracle worker."

"It would take a miracle to get Gabrielle to look at him twice," Ginger said.

"What makes him think that you can do this, Karen?" Roni asked. "Just because you write the Dear Bobby column doesn't make you a real-life Dear Bobby."

"And you're not exactly the most experienced of us with boys, are you?" Justine said. "I mean, if he'd wanted me to help him I could understand it, after all my experiences at Sagebrush Academy and with European men. . . ."

"Justine, shut up!" Roni laughed and threw her towel at her.

"That landed in my punch!" Justine squealed. "You splashed punch on me. Now you're going to get it!" She picked up an ice cube and flicked it in Roni's direction, hitting her neck.

"Aaaah! Now you're really going to get it!" Roni shrieked as she leaped up. Justine squealed and ran away, Roni following right behind her even when Justine leaped into the pool.

"Not my hair! Roni, don't get my hair wet—I

just styled it," we heard Justine shrieking, then there were flailing arms and lots of water splashing around and it was hard to tell who was who.

Ginger looked at me. "We might as well join them," she said. "It's too darned hot out here. I need to cool off."

She ran to the edge and dove in. I jumped in after her. I'm not much of a diver, or a swimmer either. To tell the truth, I don't even like getting water splashed in my face, but I wanted to enjoy being one of the gang again.

"Look at me," Justine snapped. She turned to Ginger and me. "My hair is totally ruined."

"We'll fix it for you later, Justine," Roni said. "We'll have a hair-styling session when it gets cooler. Right now, wet hair feels great."

"It sure does," Ginger said, lying on her back and floating.

"Where are the rafts, Justine?" Roni asked.

"In the pool house," Justine said. "I guess I'll get them, even though you don't really deserve one for being so mean to me."

"I wasn't mean to you. How was I mean to you?"

"You started it."

"What did I start?"

Justine thought. "I forget now. Oh, well, never mind." She climbed out and threw in four plastic rafts. We climbed on them and lay there with our hands and feet trailing in the cool water.

"This is great," Ginger said. "Finally I'm relaxed."

"I wish I could relax," I said. "I'm still so shaken up about Adam."

"If you really want him for yourself, you should try getting a new image," Justine said. "And you could start with that swimsuit. It's totally blah. You know Adam likes sexy women."

"Thanks for your vote of confidence," I said, smoothing down my black one-piece. "It happens to be the only kind of swimsuit my mother will let me wear. And as for Adam, I'm not interested anymore. If he wants Gabrielle, then he deserves her. It would serve him right if I did get them together. She'd make his life totally miserable."

"I don't see how you'd ever get her to be interested in him," Ginger said.

"Unless you lied," Roni added.

"And?"

"And told her that he was really the heir to the Queen of England in disguise, or his father was Harrison Ford."

"She'd never believe it. Remember, she's the news editor. She'd look those things up for herself."

"We are the Boyfriend Club," Justine said. "We have had experience in getting people together."

"It's never really worked, Justine," I reminded her. "Every time we've tried to get two people together, it's been a hopeless failure."

"I wouldn't say that," Justine said.

"I would," Ginger agreed. "The only time any of us have wound up with boyfriends, it's been in spite of the Boyfriend Club, not because of it."

"But we have come up with some neat ideas," Justine said. "It wasn't our fault that they never worked. I think we should put our great minds to work and come up with some ideas for Karen."

"I'd appreciate any help I could get, guys," I said.

"What would Dear Bobby say?" Roni asked.

"I wrote an answer, but that was before I knew that Adam had written the question. I told him he'd have to do something pretty special to make her notice him. I said that no girl can resist a romantic hero."

"And how do you think you can turn Adam into a romantic hero?" Ginger demanded.

"Flowers," Justine suggested. "Flowers always work with me. Send her a huge bouquet of red roses every day for a week."

"That costs megabucks, Justine," Roni reminded her.

Justine shrugged. "He has to be prepared to make sacrifices if he wants to impress her."

"Maybe he doesn't have your kind of money,

Justine," Roni said. "I couldn't come up with thirty dollars a day."

"Maybe he can splurge on one bouquet of roses," I said. "And sign it 'from a secret admirer.'"

"That's good, Karen," Justine said. "Remember when I did that at the valentine's dance to get you guys back together again? It worked, didn't it?"

"Yeah," Ginger said. "Secret admirers are mysterious and romantic. Maybe he could keep it up all week—flowers on Monday, a poem on Tuesday, a bag of Hershey's Kisses on Wednesday . . . By the end of the week she'll be dying to know who it is."

"And then she finds out it's Adam and says, 'Oh, no, not you!'" I sighed.

Roni sat up with difficulty, trying to keep her raft from tipping over. "Okay, let's be realistic. If he doesn't have the looks or the money to impress her, then he has to do something to make him look like a hero to her. After all, he does look a little like Superman when he was Clark Kent."

"That's true," I said. A sharp image of Adam's face flashed across my mind. I hadn't realized until now just how much I liked him—or wanted to like him.

"But I don't think he can leap tall buildings in a single bound, can he?" Justine asked. "Or stop speeding locomotives?"

"We could set him up to look like a hero," Roni said.

"How?" I asked.

Roni shrugged. "It will need some thinking through, of course, but there must be some way."

"I know." Justine tried to sit up too, lost her balance, and disappeared under the water.

"What were you going to say," Roni asked as Justine surfaced again, spluttering, "before you did that impressive dive? Or were you demonstrating how Gabrielle was going to drown right before Adam saved her?"

"Shut up," Justine said, but she was laughing. "I was going to say that we get Gabrielle trapped somewhere and have Adam rescue her."

"Like where, Justine?" Ginger asked.

"Some high place—a church tower, a balcony— and she won't be able get down."

"Why not?" Ginger went on.

"Because . . . because we lock the door behind her. That's right. We ask her to come up to some high place because there's a good news story up there and then we lock the door and Adam climbs up the outside of the building and rescues her."

"I see some serious flaws in this, Justine," Ginger said.

"Like what?"

"For example, what if Adam can't climb up the building? What if he's afraid of heights?"

"And what if he drops her halfway down?" I finished for her.

"At least you won't have her to worry about any longer." Roni laughed. "Sorry, but it's a crummy idea, Justine."

"Okay, so like you suggested, she's drowning and he dives in and rescues her," Justine went on.

"She's probably a better swimmer than he is," I said. "Face it, Justine, Adam is not exactly the hero type."

"Then we're all wasting our time," Justine said. "Let's get dried off and go make ice-cream sundaes. And then you get—ta-da—a tuba concert."

"I can't wait," Roni said with a big, phony smile that made Ginger and me start giggling.

"Hey, Karen," Roni whispered to me as we climbed out of the pool. "Do you really think she can play the tuba already?"

"I doubt it."

Roni glanced at Justine's disappearing back. "You have to hand it to Justine. When she wants something, she really goes after it in a big way."

I nodded. "Maybe I should try to be more like her," Roni said. "I'm dying to go out with Josh, and even though he knows I like him, all he ever says to me is, 'Hi, Roni, how's it going?'"

"That's a start," I said. "Gabrielle doesn't even say that to Adam, but he wants to believe he's got a chance with her."

"Are you really going to suggest some of these things to him?"

"I have to. I promised him I'd help, although I can't see any of them working with Gabrielle."

Roni wrapped a towel around her head and rubbed furiously. "Guys have it so easy," she said. "They can do stuff like send flowers or cards with hearts on them and girls think it's great. What can girls send?"

I shrugged. "Pizza and tickets to football games?"

Roni laughed. "The trouble is that most guys don't like to be chased by girls. They run a mile if a girl's hanging around them. Girls are flattered. They like that sort of stuff."

"Remind me," I said. "It's been so long since it happened."

Roni gave an understanding smile. "You'll find another boy soon," she said. "And this time it will be the right one, not a guy who has serious flaws, like being attracted to blond airheads."

"But that's the problem," I started. "She's not an airhead. She's blond and beautiful and smart, too. You should see her at newspaper meetings. She comes up with great ideas."

Roni sat on the bench and dried her toes. "Life is so unfair sometimes," she said. "Oh, well, let's concentrate on your task with Adam this week, and next week you can help me get somewhere with Josh. I'm even prepared to try turning into Wonder Woman and rescuing him from a burning building."

"Hey, that's not such a bad idea," I said. "We set someplace on fire and have Adam rescue Gabrielle."

Roni stood up and shook her head. "Now you've finally flipped, Karen. Set someplace on fire? The Boyfriend Club can't start doing criminal activities just to get a guy and girl together."

I grinned as we headed toward the house. "Just a thought," I said.

"The stuff's on the counter, all ready for build-your-own sundaes," Justine called.

We came through into the spotless white kitchen and stopped. She wasn't kidding. The whole counter was piled with five flavors of ice cream, hot fudge topping, butterscotch topping, blueberry topping, nuts, sprinkles, M&M's, whipped cream . . . the works.

"What did you do, buy an ice-cream store?" Roni demanded.

"Don't knock it," Ginger called. She was already piling her plate high.

"I'm having a banana split," Roni said. "How about you, Karen?"

The trauma of the ice-cream parlor came back painfully. "Uh, no thanks. I'm not into banana splits," I said.

"Hurry up, you guys," Justine said impatiently. "When you're ready, we can take the sundaes upstairs and I'll play for you."

"You're sure that won't put us off our food?" Ginger asked.

Justine made a face. "My teacher said I was making rapid progress, so there."

We followed her up the stairs.

"Where's Alexandra?" Roni asked. "I just have to hug that cute baby."

"I think she's taking a nap right now," Justine said. "Christine said we should let her sleep. We'll go see if she's awake in a little while."

The tuba was lying on the floor of Justine's room. Actually, it took up most of Justine's floor, and she has a huge room! I had forgotten what a large instrument it was close up.

"Sit down, please," she said. "The concert will begin momentarily."

We sat. Justine put music on the music stand, then struggled to pick up the tuba and place it around herself. She put her lips to it. For a long time nothing came out. Justine's face got redder and redder. Her cheeks were like balloons. Then suddenly there was this awful deep rumbling sound, like an elephant with a stomachache! It got louder and louder until the china ornaments on Justine's shelves quivered.

Justine put down the tuba. "There," she said. "What do you think of that?"

"Was that it?" Roni asked.

"Hey, that was pretty good for one lesson," Justine said. "I figure if I can get one more note each time, I'll be playing 'Mary Had a Little Lamb' any day now."

From the next room came a loud wail.

"At least it did one thing." Roni laughed, jumping up. "It woke Alexandra for us."

Chapter 9

Adam was waiting for me as I arrived at school on Monday morning.

"So?" he said. "Did you have a chance to think about what I asked you? Any brilliant ideas yet? When do we put the great plan into action?"

His face was alight and eager, like a kid's on Christmas morning. I felt a big stab of misery that his face didn't light up like that for me, but for someone who didn't deserve him. There was no way I was ever going to let him know how I felt.

"We've got a few ideas," I said smoothly. "I'm not sure how great they are, but they're a start. This isn't going to be easy, you know. Gabrielle is . . . uh . . . very choosy when it comes to guys. Look how she keeps giving Steve the brush-off, and he's both good looking *and* a superjock."

"I know." Adam sighed. "I know I probably don't stand a chance with her, but I've got to try. I feel like one of those old knights, out to win the hand of a fair lady by going on impossible quests."

"I'm sure we could lay on a dragon if you really wanted one," I said dryly.

He picked up my sarcasm and the hopeful smile melted from his face. "You think this is dumb, don't you? You think I'll be making a fool of myself."

"Who you decide to fall in love with is up to you," I said. "I just don't want you to get hurt."

"Oh, don't worry about me. I'm tougher than I look," he said. "So when do I start?"

I glanced at the clock on the wall. "We haven't really got time to talk now. I still have to put my stuff in my locker and the bell's about to ring. We'll talk after chemistry, okay?"

"Okay," he said. "I just hope the morning goes quickly. I'm dying of suspense."

If I wasn't such a nice person, I thought as I stomped away and crammed things into my locker, *I'd come up with the world's worst ideas for you, Adam Bateman, and I'd watch you make a fool of yourself—which you're probably going to do anyway.*

All through the morning I kept imagining really dumb things for Adam to do. In orchestra I thought that he could serenade Gabrielle outside her bedroom window. And since he couldn't play the violin, I'd play it in the bushes and he'd just pretend.

In math I decided that we'd set up a Brain of Alta Mesa contest, and I'd give him all the answers in advance so that he was just perfect—hey, that wasn't such a bad idea, except that Gabrielle probably thought that superbrains were all geeks.

In chemistry class Adam kept looking across at me and giving me hopeful grins, which was really annoying. He even passed me a note: GIVE ME A HINT. I frowned at him. I was in enough trouble in that class without being caught passing notes.

"Okay," I said the moment the bell rang for lunch recess. "Let's go somewhere we can talk and I'll tell you what we came up with."

"Fine. Let's go." He followed me like a puppy dog.

We sat together on the low wall that ran around the administration building. There were tall shrubs planted around the building and the wall was shady.

"All right," I said slowly, "this is the general idea. We get her interested before she knows who you are. That way she can't reject you right away."

"And how do we get her interested in me?"

"Remember she was complaining that there were no more romantic guys around at this school? Maybe you can be that romantic guy she's looking for."

"How?"

"My friends thought that you should send her flowers and sign a card from a secret admirer. All girls love getting flowers—roses if possible, but I know they're expensive."

"Flowers, that's good," Adam said. "And a secret admirer. I like that too. This is great, Karen."

"Maybe you could send her something every day this week. Flowers tomorrow, Hershey's Kisses the next day, a poem the day after that, and then by the end of the week, she'll be dying to know who you are."

"And what if she finds out it's me and she's disappointed, or mad, or even worse, she laughs?"

I'd been thinking the same thing, but I didn't want to tell him so. "That's why we decided that when she does find out who you are, she's got to be impressed."

"What could I do that would impress her?" he asked. "I'm not exactly the world's biggest jock. I'm certainly not rich. I don't drive a fast car—I don't actually drive any car yet. I don't even have my permit. What would impress a girl like Gabrielle?"

"Saving her life?"

"Yeah, I guess that might do it," he said, then he laughed. "Come on, Karen. Just how do you think I'm going to save her life?"

"We set up something to make it look like she's in danger, and then you step in and rescue her."

"Like what, for example?"

"My friends thought about getting her trapped somewhere high up and then having you climb up the building and carry her down to safety."

"Me? Climb up a building?"

"Yeah. I thought it was a dumb idea, too," I said.

"We could always have someone dress up as a mugger and jump out at her in the dark, and I could fight him off," Adam said.

"And what if she screams and the police come and there's a big scene?"

He nodded. "This isn't going to be easy, is it? Are you sure that acting like a hero is the best way to impress her?"

"What other ways can you think of?" I asked. "You've just said you're not a jock and you're not rich and you're not exactly built like Arnold yet."

"That's it!" Adam yelled. "I could go to the gym and start pumping iron. She thinks of me as nerdy Adam, but one day I reveal that under this nerdy exterior is a body of steel. I rip off my T-shirt and there are all these fantastic muscles. . . ." He paused, waiting for me to say something. I couldn't say anything because my lips were pressed together so that I didn't laugh. "Well, what do you think?" he demanded.

"It's a great idea, Adam, if you're prepared to wait a year for her and spend that whole year at the gym."

"You don't think I can get pumped up in a week?"

I shook my head.

"A month?"

"I doubt it."

"So the whole thing's really hopeless, isn't it?" he said. He sat there on the wall, staring out in front of him, and I couldn't help feeling sorry for him. I knew that I should be mad at him, but I wanted to put my arm around his shoulders and promise to make everything all right.

"Let's start out with the secret admirer part," I said. "Who knows, it just might work."

"Okay, I'll do it," he said. "Flowers and a card signed Secret Admirer. I'll buy them tonight and bring them in tomorrow. We've got a newspaper meeting after school. I can put them in her place for her to find."

"Make sure you put them in water if they're going to be here all day."

He nodded. "Good thinking. Then I'll sprint up to the newspaper office and take them out of the water before she gets there." He got to his feet. "This is going to be so great. I can't wait."

We started walking back to our lockers.

"Thanks for doing this for me, Karen," he said. "I really appreciate it."

"Always glad to help a friend," I managed to say.

"I'm really glad we've become such good friends," he said.

This one took even more concentration. I took a deep breath before I said, "Me, too."

"You want to eat lunch with me?"

"I always eat lunch with my friends Roni, Ginger, and Justine," I said. "We meet under our tree."

"Oh, okay. See you around, then. I'll show you the flowers tomorrow morning."

I wished he'd go. This was turning out to be more stressful than I had thought.

The first thing I saw when I got to school the next morning was Adam's beaming face. "I got them," he said. "Do you want to see?"

"Where are they?"

"I asked Mr. Parnow if I could put them in the room at the back of the chemistry lab. Come on, I'll show you."

I followed him down the hall.

"I hope she's going to like them," he said. "You're sure this is a good idea? She's not going to be mad at me?"

"I told you, all girls like getting flowers," I said.

We were just passing my locker when I noticed a figure step out of the shadows. It didn't take much brainwork to guess that it was Jeremy, hanging around my locker again. Usually he'd go away if I ignored him. This time he stepped out, barring my way.

"Hi, Karen," he said.

I was very conscious of Adam beside me.

"Hi, Jeremy," I said flatly.

He whipped something from behind his back. "Flowers. For you," he said.

I was speechless. All I could do was stand there, staring at the flowers. They were definitely what you might call a mixed bunch—daisies and petunias and furry stuff and even a sprig of oleander. They made the weirdest bouquet I had ever seen, and it was pretty obvious that they'd been living in someone's front yard until a few minutes earlier.

"Jeremy . . ." I stammered.

Jeremy was grinning hopefully. "Owen and Ronald got them for me this morning. They said all girls like flowers, and I wanted to give you some as a token of my love."

All that was going through my brain was that Adam might actually think the creep and I were an item—and I wouldn't have wanted my worst enemy to get that impression.

I thrust the flowers back at him. "Jeremy, how many times do I have to tell you that I don't want tokens of your love?" I said. "I don't want your love, period. Please take them away and throw them in a garbage can before the cops cite you for digging up someone's yard."

"They were in a public park," Jeremy said in a hurt voice. "And my parents are taxpayers and Ronald said they were growing too close together and needed thinning anyway." He gazed at me hopefully. "I'll get you roses if you like. . . ."

"No . . . uh . . . thank you," I stammered. "No roses. No daisies. No songs. No symphonies. If you really want to please me . . ."

"Yes?"

"Just leave me alone, okay? I don't want to hurt you, but I'm just not interested—and I never will be."

I grabbed Adam's sleeve. "Come on, Adam. What did you want to show me?"

We walked past Jeremy and his flowers and into the lab. Adam had gone very pale. "Didn't you say all girls like getting flowers," he said in a shaky voice.

"They do, ninety-nine percent of the time," I said. "When the flowers don't look like weeds and they weren't just stolen from a local park and they're not delivered by a nerd."

"What if she thinks my flowers look like weeds and she thinks I'm a nerd?"

"Adam, don't worry about it. I might have liked the flowers if they'd come from someone else. It's just that this guy has been bugging me all year. He won't take no for an answer. He's driving me crazy. He can't get it into his head that I don't like him."

Adam sighed. "I wonder if Gabrielle will say the same thing about me."

"No way. You're not a nerd and you're not annoying. I'm sure she'll like your flowers. Did you get roses like I suggested?"

He shook his head. "They were way too much money. I got a mixed bouquet."

"I see," I said. It was possible that Adam was already doomed. If the flowers looked anything like the bouquet I had just been given, I didn't think that Gabrielle would be too impressed. I was prepared for the worst as we went into the chemistry lab, but then I was looking at a perfect bunch of delicate flowers in soft pastel shades. They were even prettier than roses. I felt tears welling up at the back of my eyes.

"They're lovely, Adam," I muttered. "Any girl would love to get flowers like that. I'm sure she'll like them."

I really didn't want to go to the newspaper staff meeting after school, but I couldn't think of a good excuse not to be there. Besides, Adam told me that he needed my support.

"I don't know if I can bear to watch when she sees the flowers," he said. "Would you be there for me?"

"But she'll suspect something if you're the only person not there."

"What if I turn bright red when she looks at me?"

"You have to handle some of this yourself, Adam," I snapped. My patience was wearing kind of thin. Helping set him up with my least favorite person in the universe was bad enough. Watching her oohing over his flowers and reporting it to him was too much.

"You're right," he said. "I'm already asking you to do a lot for me." He grabbed my arm. "But I promise I'll make it up to you sometime. I'll do something really special for you someday. I'll beat up your annoying nerd for you, if you like—after I've started pumping iron."

"Tempting, but no thanks."

"I'll help set you up with the guy of your dreams if you want."

"You can't do that," I blurted.

"Why not?"

"Because . . . because there's no guy of my dreams right now."

"There will be," he said. "You're a very special girl, Karen. Any guy would be lucky to get you." His eyes smiled encouragingly into mine. "Here we are," he said. We had reached the newspaper office door. "Wish me luck, Karen."

"Good luck, Adam," I whispered.

We arrived at least five seconds before Gabrielle.

We hadn't even sat down when we heard her voice echoing down the hallway. "So I told the little creep to stay out of my way if he knew what was good for him, and he said . . ." She stopped.

"Ooh, look, flowers," Gabrielle's friend Margie exclaimed. "I wonder who they're for? There's a note on them. Hey, Gabrielle, they're for you!"

Gabrielle looked at the flowers, then picked up the card and ripped it open. "My secret admirer," she said out loud. "Give me a break." She looked around the room. "Okay, which of you clowns did this? Don't tell me this is the kind of thing you'd do, Steve Garcia," she said.

"Me? No way," Steve said. "I don't waste my money on flowers, baby. When I want a girl, I snap my fingers and they *all* come running."

"In your dreams," Gabrielle said. "Well, I'd love to know who it was."

Adam glanced at me and grinned. But then Gabrielle went on, "It's certainly not one of my close friends. If it was anyone who knew me at all, they'd know that I have bad hay fever and I'm desperately allergic to anything but roses." She handed the flowers to Margie. "Here, take these and get them out of here before I start sneezing."

Adam instantly turned bright red. But it didn't matter. Gabrielle never once looked in his direction.

Chapter 10

"Strike one," Adam said to me as soon as we were far enough away from the newspaper office.

"Sorry," I said. "How was I to know she's the one girl in the world who is allergic to flowers?"

"So what do we do now?"

I thought for a moment. "We go on with the plan. Even if she didn't like the flowers, I bet she's dying to know who her secret admirer is. Send her a card tomorrow saying that you're looking forward to meeting her soon—find one of those cards that's really mushy. You know, 'You're so special to me. You make my life worth living. You make the sun come up in the morning. . . .' That kind of stuff."

Adam had taken out a little notebook. "You make the sun come up in the morning," he repeated slowly

119

as he wrote it down. "This is all good stuff, Karen. Could you come help me choose a card?"

"No, thanks," I said. I was thinking that I'd want to choose a card that read, "I'd love to send you flowers, but I don't think they grow Venus's flytraps big enough," or even "I wish you well . . . if I can find one deep enough." Okay, so I wasn't trying that hard to be understanding. I knew well enough that love was a funny thing. You couldn't always pick the person you fell in love with. Sometimes a person was right for you and it was great and sometimes— wham, it was like being struck by lightning. There was nothing you could do about it. And I suspected that Adam knew as well as I did that Gabrielle wasn't the most suitable person for him.

"Please come," he said. "I need you, Karen. You know just what kind of card a girl would like to get from the guy of her dreams. I need you to tell me what message you'd love to get in a card."

"What I'd want doesn't matter," I snapped, then I made myself cool it. "Gabrielle and I have nothing in common, Adam. That should be fairly obvious."

"Yeah, but you're both girls. You're both smart and cute, even though she's a blonde and you're a brunette. And even though she has these enormous blue eyes that kind of sparkle when she laughs and . . ."

"Would you shut up, please," I said. "I really don't appreciate being compared to Gabrielle and

120

told how much better she is than me."

"Oh, but she isn't," Adam said. "You're special, too. It's just that . . . I've got this thing for Gabrielle right now, so everything about her looks good to me."

"Just find a card that tells her she's wonderful and gorgeous, and you can't go wrong," I said.

He glanced at me suspiciously. "You don't like her, do you?"

"My opinion doesn't count, Adam. You like her and I promised I'd help you, but just don't expect me to be excited about it."

He gave a little embarrassed smile. "I'm sorry that I've been bugging you so much. It's just that you're the only person I can rely on. And it's not as if I'm asking you to do anything yourself. I only want Dear Bobby's advice."

Dear Bobby, I thought as I walked away. *That's all I am—a person who solves other people's problems. Nobody ever thinks that I might have hopes and dreams of my own.*

"So what was it tonight?" my mother asked as I let myself in the front door. "Newspaper or boy?"

"Newspaper, of course."

She snorted. "You wouldn't tell me if it was a boy, would you?"

"What is this, the Spanish Inquisition?" I snapped. "How many times do I have to tell you that I'm not meeting a boy? There is no boy in my

121

life right now. There is no boy I like. There is no boy who likes me. Okay? Satisfied?"

"If you say so," she said flatly. "That's not what I've been hearing."

"What have you been hearing? From who?"

She tapped her finger to her nose. "A little bird," she said. "And I want to tell you, it's okay with me. You don't have to pretend you're working at a newspaper every afternoon. You can bring him home to meet us."

"Mom. There isn't a boy. Why won't you believe me? Whoever your 'little bird' is, he or she is dead wrong! Now can we drop this?" I stormed off, shouting over my shoulder, "I'm going to do my homework. Bye."

It was hard to decide which was more annoying right now, home or school. I wondered what was going on in my mother's head and where she got the idea that I was keeping a boy secret from her. I had spent the last year fighting with my parents because they thought I was too young to have a boy-friend. Now it seemed I was fighting with them because I didn't have one and they thought I did. "Little bird." Whom had she been talking to?

"I found the perfect card!" Adam was waiting by my locker first thing Tuesday morning. It seemed this was becoming a daily ritual: Adam filled with excitement over the latest nice thing he was going to do for a girl who would never appreciate it or him. All I wanted to do now was get him together with Gabrielle as quickly as possible so that all this would stop. I remembered that Justine had suggested paying Gabrielle to go on a date with him. Suddenly even that didn't sound like such a dumb idea. I found myself wondering how much money it would actually take—I must have been in major stress overload.

"Look," Adam said, taking the card from its envelope and shoving it under my nose. "You have to admit it's just perfect. It even looks like her."

On the front of the card was a girl who did look a lot like Gabrielle. She was standing in the middle of nature, surrounded by birds and cute little furry animals, and the words said, "You make every day special with your wonderful smile."

I wished Justine was here. She was great at doing fake gagging noises.

"So what do you think?" he asked excitedly.

"It's fine if she's not allergic to fur and feathers. Have you written a message inside it yet?"

He shook his head. "I was waiting to see if you thought the card was okay."

I opened it, then I started laughing.

"Karen? What's the matter?"

"You were intending to send this card to Gabrielle?"

"Yes," Adam replied shyly.

123

"And you didn't think to look inside it?"

"The front was just right. What's so funny?"

I waved the card triumphantly in his face. "It says 'To a special daughter.'"

He snatched it from me. "What? You've got to be joking. Oh, no." His face had turned beet red. "I am so embarrassed. How dumb of me. Can you imagine her face if she'd gotten this?"

I couldn't stop laughing. "She'd think her parents had just dropped by to remind her how much they love her."

"You see," he said, waving the card at me. "I can't do a thing right without you. I need your help, Karen. You've got to talk me through this. I can't risk another catastrophe. So tell me, where do I go from here?"

"You could exchange that card for a better one tonight," I said. "Only make sure you read the inside first."

"Or?"

"I guess you could move on to do another gift. I get the feeling that Gabrielle is the kind who likes getting things. Who doesn't?" I added.

"So you think maybe candy? A big box of chocolates?"

"Something more romantic," I said. "How about a big box of Hershey's Kisses?"

"Perfect," he said. "I'll get my mom to drive me to the wholesale warehouse and I can buy the industrial-size bags of Hershey's Kisses."

124

"Industrial-size Hershey's Kisses. That sounds so romantic," I teased.

His eyes met mine. "You know what I mean," he said.

I wished he wouldn't look at me like that. Most of the time I could tell myself that I wasn't interested in him any longer. But when his eyes smiled into mine like that, it was hard to remember that I was just Dear Bobby to him.

"Don't forget to put them in a pretty box," I said. "She won't be too thrilled if she gets a plain plastic bag dumped in front of her."

He nodded. "I know. I think I can handle this one. I'll show you what I've bought in the morning."

And Wednesday morning he was waiting for me again.

"So what do you think? Is it just right?" he asked, holding open a grocery bag. I looked inside. The box was like an old-fashioned hatbox, decorated with Impressionist pictures. It was very heavy, obviously filled to the top with Hershey's Kisses .

"It's wonderful, Adam. She'd be crazy if she wasn't impressed by this."

"I hope so," he said. "I really hope this works. The stress is getting to me. I can't sleep nights, just thinking about her."

I was holding the bag and secretly hoping that

Gabrielle would eat all those kisses at one session and blow up instantly to a huge size or, better still, break out in acne all over her face. I guess that deep down I'm not a very nice person.

"I'm going to put it in the newspaper office after lunch," he said. "That way nobody can raid the box before Gabrielle gets it."

Because we had spent all of Monday's meeting reviewing the first issue of the newspaper, Brad had scheduled an extra meeting to try to make progress on our second issue. I couldn't help being curious as I climbed the stairs to the newspaper room after school was out. I hoped the kisses would work as much as Adam did, because I was running out of ideas.

Gabrielle wasn't there when Adam and I arrived and took our places at the table.

"Is your second column ready yet, Karen?" Brad asked.

"Uh . . . almost." I had been so caught up with Adam's problem that I'd sort of forgotten I had a real column to write.

"What's that box doing on the table?" Brad asked.

Margie looked at it. "It's for Gabrielle," she said. "I bet it's from her secret admirer again. How romantic. She's so lucky." She looked up as Gabrielle came into the room. "He's sent you another present, Gabrielle," she called. "Get over here and see what it is. We're all dying to know."

"What is this?" Gabrielle asked, and I was delighted to see that she was blushing. "It isn't my birthday. It isn't Valentine's Day. Is this some sort of stunt, do you think? I don't want to find out that I'm on "Candid Camera" when I'm not having a good hair day."

"There's a card on top, Gabrielle," Margie squealed. "Open it."

"Okay, okay." She opened the card. "You're right. From my secret admirer again. Well, I like his taste in boxes."

"What's inside?" Margie urged.

Gabrielle took off the lid. Her eyes narrowed. "This has to be some sort of joke," she said. She glared at Steve. "Are you sure this isn't from you?"

"Hey, don't look at me. I had nothing to do with it," he growled.

"Well, either it's a joke or it has to be from a total stranger or an idiot," Gabrielle said. "I've been on a diet for as long as I can remember and I haven't eaten a single piece of candy all year." She took the box and handed it to Brad. "Here, pass it around. Everyone take a handful. Help yourselves, because I'm not eating any."

Adam's eyes caught mine as the box came our way. "Have some chocolate, Karen." He passed me the half-empty box.

Chapter

11

I walked home deep in thought. I was feeling bad for Adam and mad at myself for having let him down. Now what was I going to do? I'd have to wait for the Saturday night sleepover and see if my friends could come up with any brilliant ideas.

I opened the front door and was met with the most delicious cooking smell. My mother was in the kitchen, surrounded by piles of chopped vegetables, egg roll wrappers, chicken breasts, and sliced pork. Dumplings were simmering in broth.

"What's this all about?" I asked.

"Guests for dinner," Mom said. "Wash your hands and you can help me. They'll be here in an hour."

"Guests? Who? We never have guests on a

weeknight." Actually we hardly ever had guests, period. My mother was very shy about her cooking skills, so the only people we entertained were very close friends or my friends from school.

"You wait and see," Mom said. "A big surprise."

"Who? Someone I know?"

"Yes," she said. "I told you, wait and be surprised. And while you're waiting, help me wrap these egg rolls."

I helped her cook for a while, then she glanced at the clock. "Go change into something nicer. Put on a dress. We don't entertain guests wearing jeans."

"Oh, Mom. Do I have to eat with you? I've got a ton of stuff to do."

"Of course you eat with us. I've cooked a very special meal. You're going to be very pleased that your mother cares so much about you and wants you to be happy."

I had no idea what she was talking about, but I went and changed into a summer dress anyway. I just hoped our guests weren't the sort of friends who patted me on the head and told me I'd grown and asked me what I wanted to be when I grew up. And I hoped I didn't have to speak Vietnamese all evening, because I wasn't very good at it.

By six o'clock the table was set with the best

silverware and fresh flowers. My mother jumped when the doorbell rang.

"Answer it, please, Karen."

"Me?"

"Yes, you. Go on, quick."

I went to the front door, rapidly going through the Vietnamese words for "Hello, how are you, I'm very well."

I opened the door and all words, in any language, went completely out of my head. Jeremy was standing there with a big bouquet of roses in his arms.

"Hi, Karen," he said.

"Jeremy? What are you doing here?" It came out as a squeak. "How did you find out where I live?"

"We all exchanged addresses at camp, remember?" he said, smiling at my embarrassment.

"Look, I'm sorry, but you can't come in right now," I said, glancing back at the kitchen. "My mother is expecting guests for dinner any moment."

Any second now she'd come out and get the wrong idea about Jeremy, especially after all those questions about secret boyfriends.

"I know," he said. "It's me. I'm the guest."

"You? My mother invited you for dinner? Here?"

He was still smiling as if he'd pulled off something really clever. "Aren't you going to invite me in? I brought you flowers."

My mother appeared from the kitchen at this moment. "Ah, Jeremy, you got here. Please come in. Karen, invite him in. And you brought such lovely flowers, too."

I looked from my mother's face to Jeremy's. I was feeling as if I'd just stepped into a parallel nightmare universe.

"How do you two know each other?" I stammered.

"Jeremy stopped by to visit you last Saturday, when you were over at your friend's house," she said. "He told me all about how you two met at music camp. He said that you two are the best of friends. . . ."

"He said what?"

My mother had put her hand on Jeremy's arm and was dragging him inside like a prize catch. "So I think to myself," she went on talking, "that this young man is a nice boy, a musician, a boy your father and I approve of. Why do you keep him hidden from us?"

"Mom, Jeremy and I are just . . . uh . . . friends," I managed to blurt. It was hard even to say the word *friends,* but I could hardly tell her the truth— that I'd rather be friends with a giant tarantula. Well, maybe not. I don't like spiders.

My mother was still smiling from ear to ear, as if she were a magician who had just pulled off some amazing trick. "Jeremy tells me he's a first-class musician," she said knowingly. "He wants to play in an orchestra someday. He thinks you should take your music more seriously, like we do."

I was now experiencing one of the problems of having been brought up polite. Even though I was hopping mad, I just couldn't yell at my mother, not with a stranger present.

"Uh . . . would you excuse me a second?" I managed to say politely. "I have to make a very important phone call. I'll be right back."

"Hurry up," Mom said. "Your father will be home any minute, and then we eat."

"I hope I'm not too early, Mrs. Nguyen," I heard Jeremy say in his all-too-familiar creepy voice.

"Not at all. Now you and Karen can have some time talking before we eat, huh?"

I fled to my room. My fingers were shaking so much I found it hard to dial Justine's number. "Please be home," I prayed.

"Hello?" It was Justine's voice.

"Justine? It's Karen. Listen, I'm in big trouble. I need you to get over here right now."

"Right now? Karen, I'm in the middle of feeding Alex her applesauce. Then I'm going to bathe her."

"Is Christine out?"

"No, she's here. I just like doing it," Justine said.

"Justine, this is a real emergency," I said. "You'll never guess who just got here. Jeremy."

"Jeremy's at your house?"

"Right. And guess what? My mother invited him for dinner. She thinks we have a secret thing going."

"Why would she think that?"

"Because that's what Jeremy told her. And she thinks he's a wonderful boy and a good influence on me, too. So she's doing everything she can to encourage him."

"No way!"

"Justine, you're the only thing that could save this evening from total disaster. If you're not here, I know that I'll explode and be rude to everyone and then I'll be in big trouble. And this could be your big chance to let Jeremy get to know you better. And my mom's cooked this whole banquet."

"Don't go on. You've convinced me. I'll be right over," Justine said. "I'll see if Christine can drive me. I'll say it's a real emergency, which it is."

"Thanks, Justine." I let out a sigh of relief as I put down the phone. I even managed a smile as I went back into the living room.

"Jeremy was telling me about all the fun you had at music camp," my mother said. She looked really

134

happy. "He tells me you went for long walks in the forest together."

"We went for long walks in the forest, but not together," I said. I could remember those walks clearly. . . . It was me and a girl called Anita Robinson and then, a few yards behind us, Jeremy. And we kept turning around and saying, "Would you quit following us like that?"

"Hardly romantic," I added.

Jeremy didn't even have the grace to blush. He was still grinning at me like an idiot.

"Oh, Dad's home," I said, leaping up. I was glad for any excuse to get away. "Hi, Dad. How was your day?"

He looked at me suspiciously. Usually I didn't act hyper around him.

"Her young man is here, Francis," my mother called to him. "Come and say hello to Jeremy."

My father came into the living room and shook hands shyly. "Always glad to meet my daughter's friends," he said.

"This is a special friend. The one I told you about—the good musician who hopes to go to the conservatory next year."

Ah, so that was it. She hoped that Jeremy would be able to persuade me to go to the conservatory with him. Talk about sneaky. I looked at the clock. Where the heck was Justine? What if her stepmother wouldn't drive her and she had to ride her bike or take a bus?

"Let's go eat," my father said. "I'm starving. How about you, Jeremy?"

"Oh, yes, very hungry, thank you, sir. And it smells delicious."

"All Vietnamese specialties," Mom said. "I think you'll like them."

We sat at the table. I showed Jeremy how to use chopsticks and was glad when he dropped his egg roll on the middle of the tablecloth. At last the doorbell rang. I jumped up. "I'll get it," I said.

I sprinted to the front door. "Boy, am I glad to see you," I whispered to Justine. "We're at dinner. Come on in and act surprised."

I led her through to the dining room. "Look who just stopped by. You remember Justine, don't you, Mom and Dad? Jeremy, do you remember Justine?"

"I . . . uh . . . think so," he said, looking at her uneasily. So the nerds had warned him about her, then. I just hoped they hadn't done too much damage.

"Justine stopped by to work on homework together," I said. "But as you can see, we're eating dinner. I know, why don't you join us? We've got enough, haven't we, Mom?"

My mother spread her hands. "We have plenty, but I thought . . ."

"Great. Grab a chair, Justine. Here. Pull it up between Jeremy and me."

Justine sat and smiled at Jeremy.

"So, Jeremy, you're in the orchestra at school, right?" she asked.

"That's correct."

"And you play the . . . uh . . . long black thing that you blow . . . the saxophone?"

"Clarinet," he said crushingly.

"That's right. I always get those two mixed up." She giggled. I didn't think she'd made a very good start.

"I might be joining the orchestra too," she went on happily. "If I can fit it in along with the marching band."

"You play an instrument?" He looked surprised.

"Oh, yes."

"Justine plays the tuba," I said.

"The tuba. Amazing. Isn't that very hard for a girl?"

"Not for a girl with lungs like mine," Justine said. "I can play as well as any guy."

"How long have you been studying?"

"Uh . . ."

"Quite a while," I interrupted. "She's been studying for a while. She's been considering taking lessons with the tuba player from the Boston Pops."

"I had no idea you were a musician, too,"

Jeremy said. "Who is your favorite composer?"

I held my breath.

"Beethoven," she said.

"Mine, too," Jeremy exclaimed. "Which symphony do you like best?"

Justine shot me an anxious look. I held up nine fingers under the tablecloth.

"Uh . . . the tenth." I clamped down on my little finger. "No, sorry, make that ninth," she stammered.

Jeremy laughed. "The tenth. What a kidder."

"What's wrong with the tenth?"

I kicked her under the table.

"Beethoven only wrote nine symphonies," Jeremy said dryly.

"Oh, yes, silly me. I was thinking of Bach."

"He didn't write any symphonies."

"He didn't? What did he write, then?"

I had to step in before she totally blew her chances.

"Justine has been to lots of concerts in Europe."

"Really? La Scala?"

"Oh, yes. I heard her."

"It's an opera house."

"Oh."

Jeremy leaned across Justine to talk to me. "The Phoenix Symphony has a fine season this year. We have season tickets. I hope you'll come with me to the next concert. It's Mahler."

"How nice. Jeremy has invited you to a concert," my mother said. "It's okay. We give our permission to go."

"We went to a great concert last summer, didn't we, Karen?" Justine said. I realized too late what she meant. "It was the Lizards of Oz. Do you know them, Jeremy?"

"No, I don't think . . ."

"They're heavy metal."

I sighed. Justine had just doomed herself.

After dinner I announced that Justine and I had to work on a homework project. Jeremy took the hint and went.

"Thank you very much for a lovely evening," he said. "I hope Karen will be able to come to my house soon."

Not in a million years, I thought, but I didn't want to make a scene right now. Later, when Justine had gone, I'd clue my mother in and let her know that there was no way I was interested in either Jeremy or the conservatory.

"Why did you invite her to join us?" my mother whispered to me. "She spoils your chances with the young man."

I glanced across at Justine. "Not really," I muttered. If only Justine hadn't been quite so clueless, maybe she could have taken Jeremy's mind off me. As it was, it looked like I was still doomed.

Chapter

12

On Saturday night we slept over at Ginger's house. I knew it was my turn, but there was no way I was having my friends to my house. The way my mother was acting, she'd probably invite Jeremy to join us—and that thought was too terrible to bear. Jeremy in striped pajamas crashing our slumber party to play me a serenade? Aaaaaah!

So Ginger said she'd have the sleepover at her house. I got there early, just in case my mother had any more dinner party ideas. Justine arrived just after me. She was bursting with excitement as she stepped out of her father's Mercedes. "Guess what, you guys? I learned another note today. I would have brought my tuba to play it to you, but it wouldn't fit in the car. I'm going to tell Mr. Healey that I'm ready to march with the band on Friday night."

"With two notes?" I asked, taking the sleeping bag she handed me from the crammed trunk of the car. Justine didn't know the meaning of traveling light.

"Maybe I can learn a couple more notes by Friday, and anyway, tubas only need to go oompah, don't they? I'm so excited. Jeremy will have to be impressed, won't he?"

Justine never stopped amazing me. It just hadn't sunk in that she had doomed herself at my house by acting totally clueless about music. It would take a miracle to make Jeremy like her now.

It would also take a miracle to make Gabrielle like Adam. In my own dinner party trauma, I'd forgotten about him. But I remembered again as we lay on our sleeping bags later that evening.

"You guys," I said, staring up at Ginger's ceiling. "What am I going to do about Adam?"

"Give it up. It isn't working," Ginger said.

"But I promised him."

"You did your best. We always knew it was hopeless, so forget it," Justine said.

"You wouldn't like it if I told you to forget Jeremy," I reminded her.

"That's different. We have a serious chance at a beautiful relationship." She paused and glared at me as I started laughing. "You wait, Karen. When he sees me playing that tuba, he'll throw himself at my feet," Justine said. I was just trying to picture Justine staggering around with a monster tuba, tripping over Jeremy, when she added, "But Adam and Gabrielle? She doesn't even know that he's her secret admirer."

"Which is the only lucky break he's had so far," Roni commented.

"But where do we go from here? We can't risk any more gifts or cards." I sighed. "Everything I've thought of has turned out wrong."

"Then you have to go straight to plan two—the superhero," Roni said.

"Turn Adam into a superhero?" Justine spluttered. "I didn't think that the Boyfriend Club could work miracles!"

I ignored her. "What have you got in mind, Roni?"

Roni shrugged. "Some sort of dramatic rescue. That's as far as we got before, wasn't it?"

"I've been thinking and thinking, but I can't come up with any kind of dramatic rescue at our school," I said. "We don't have a tower for him to climb, and he didn't sound too excited about climbing a tower anyway."

"We could fake a robbery," Justine suggested.

"Adam thought of something like that, but it's

too risky. Someone would call the police and then we'd be in big trouble."

Ginger sat up on her bed. "It has to be a situation where only Adam can be brave. So Gabrielle has to be alone, with no help around. A fire might do it. He could rescue her from a fire."

"I thought of that, but I'm not going to risk setting the school on fire just for Adam."

Ginger grinned at me. "A fake fire, Karen. My brother used to have smoke bombs when he was a bratty little kid. He'd set one off and then yell 'Fire!' It looked pretty realistic."

"Do you think he still has any?"

"No, but he'd know where to get them. And they're quite harmless. They just make a lot of smoke. We'd need to get Gabrielle somewhere alone first."

"Wait a minute," I said excitedly. "She stays late at the newspaper office on Wednesday afternoons with Brad."

"So we'd need to get Brad out of the way, which shouldn't be too hard," Roni said. "One of us could tell him that some girl wanted to see him at the front entrance. No boy could resist that."

"Then we set off the smoke bomb," Ginger went on, "and make sure that Gabrielle is trapped. Does the office door lock?"

"It has to," I said. "There's expensive computer equipment in there."

"Great. We lock the door, Gabrielle's trapped. She screams. Adam appears dramatically from somewhere. . . ."

"There's a big closet," I said. "He could be hiding in there."

"Great. He leaps out of the closet, throws the smoke bomb out the window, and rescues her," Ginger finished.

"How?"

"We wait for the right moment and unlock the door. She'll think he's broken it down and be impressed."

"It sounds okay in theory," I said cautiously.

"Can you do better?" Ginger demanded.

I shook my head.

"Then we have to go with the best we've got," Ginger said. "It's the only thing we can come up with that isn't really dangerous but still has a chance of making Adam look good."

"I guess," I said dubiously.

Roni gave me an encouraging smile. "It just might work, and by this time next week you won't have to worry about Adam anymore."

I didn't say what I was thinking. I lay back, staring at the ceiling. For starters, I could think of all the things that could go wrong with Ginger's brilliant plan. But if it did work, if it made Gabrielle really fall for Adam . . . did I really want that to happen? I shut off a mental picture of Adam and Gabrielle walking across campus, holding hands.

I'll make it work, I decided. *I'll get them together and then he'll see what a big mistake he's made. He'll suddenly realize how dumb he's been to chase after a girl like Gabrielle when he could have had a girl like me!*

On Monday morning Adam was really excited when I told him the plan. He didn't seem to think that anything could go wrong, which shows you how crazy he was about Gabrielle . . . or maybe just plain crazy. "It's perfect, Karen. I can see it now. She'll be hammering on the door in a panic. I'll leap out of the closet and sweep her into my arms and break down the door. . . ."

"Wait a minute. How are you going to break down the door if she's in your arms?"

"Okay, so I kick down the door."

"You'd better practice that part," I said dryly. "You don't want to risk falling over with her in your arms."

"Good idea. Do you want to volunteer?"

"No, thanks," I said hastily. "I'm sure I could never play Gabrielle convincingly."

He looked at me questioningly for a second, then he grinned again. "I'll have to practice with my little sister. She won't mind. I'll tell her we're playing Mighty Morphin Power Rangers."

Adam was so cute when he was excited that I couldn't be mad at him. I guess I'd have been equally excited if my wildest dream was about to come true. Unfortunately, it wasn't about to.

By Wednesday, Ginger, Roni, Justine, and I had gone through all the details of our plan with Adam. Adam kept grinning at me in chemistry class and I kept going over all the things that could go wrong. My worst-case scenario was that someone outside the building would see the smoke before Gabrielle did and call the fire department and then we'd be in big trouble. We'd even make the next headline in the school newspaper: FIREBUGS GET THREE-DAY SUSPENSION FOR PRANK. I could imagine what my parents would say about that. They'd probably use it as an excuse to take me away from Alta Mesa and send me back to the conservatory or the world's strictest Catholic convent, with ten-foot walls around it. . . .

Think positive, I told myself. *This is excitement. This is action. If you can pull it off, you'll have achieved the impossible.* The trouble was, I couldn't see myself as a superheroine. I knew I couldn't leap over tall buildings in a single bound.

I was feeling sick to my stomach as Adam and I hurried up to the newspaper office. We made it there before Gabrielle did—a good start. I tried to make Adam a hiding place behind a stack of file boxes, but there wasn't much room in the closet to hide. If Gabrielle opened the door, she wouldn't see him right away, but if she came inside, there was no way she'd miss him. Now we just had to pray that Gabrielle didn't want anything from the closet tonight.

"Okay? You've got the smoke bomb and the matches," I said. "You know the cue for lighting the bomb. When you hear me say the word *Brad,* go ahead and light it. Give me about thirty seconds to leave and lock the door, then throw it under the table where she can't see it right away."

"Roger," Adam said coolly, looking much more nervous than he sounded.

"Okay, then. I'm going to close the door. You're *sure* you're all set?"

"I'm fine." He looked up at me, his eyes glowing. "I can't tell you how much I appreciate everything you've done for me, Karen. You're the best friend I ever had."

I shrugged. "Let's just hope this crazy plan works, Adam. Good luck. I'm going now."

I went, and just in time, too. Gabrielle and Brad were coming up the stairs as I darted into the nearest open doorway. Then I sprinted down to join Roni, Justine, and Ginger by our lockers. We waited until the halls had completely emptied. It seemed to take forever for the stream of people to stop coming out through the main doors.

"Now?" Ginger asked.

I nodded.

"Operation Adam begins," Roni said dramatically.

"How exciting. I feel like I'm in a Sylvester Stallone movie," Justine said. "All I need is my automatic weapon."

"Yeah, right." Ginger laughed. "I can just see Justine spraying bullets. She's dangerous enough without weapons."

"Let's go," Roni said. "Come on, Justine. Over to the front door. Good luck, Ginger. Good luck, Karen."

We nodded and went our separate ways. Ginger and I headed up the stairs. I waited out of sight of the newspaper office while she went ahead and opened the door. "Is there a guy named Brad in here?" she asked.

"That's me," I heard him say.

"There's some girl looking for you outside, near the front entrance," Ginger said. She did it perfectly.

"A girl? What girl? What did she look like?"

"I didn't notice too much. She said you'd be in the newspaper office but she didn't know where it was. So I said I'd come and get you."

"Thanks," Brad said. I heard a chair scrape. Then Brad said, "I'll be right back, Gabrielle."

I ducked into the shadows as Brad hurried past me. Now I just hoped that Roni and Justine could do their part. It should work okay. Roni had disguised herself so he wouldn't recognize her, and she was a terrific actress—she'd be able to come up with a good story to keep him down there long enough.

I counted to a hundred, then walked down the hall. There was a glass panel in the door and I could see Gabrielle working at her computer, her back to me. Perfect. I flung open the office door.

"Hi, is Brad here?" I asked.

"Brad? He just left," Gabrielle said. "Some girl was looking for him."

"Where did he go, do you know?"

"Front entrance, I think," Gabrielle said, already going back to her computer. Great. This was working perfectly. She wasn't even looking as I murmured "thanks" and shut the door. She certainly wasn't looking as I turned Brad's spare key.

I ducked out of sight and waited, holding my breath. If Brad appeared again too quickly, I had to detain him, but things should have started by now. Ginger said she tested a smoke bomb at home and those things sent out amazing amounts of smoke right away.

I waited and waited. Suddenly I heard a shriek. Gabrielle's voice was screaming, "Ohmygod, there's smoke coming from the closet!"

The closet? That wasn't right. I inched closer to peek in through the glass panel. She was right. Great billows of smoke were coming through the crack under the closet door. There was no sign of Adam. Something had gone terribly wrong. I couldn't wait a moment longer. I unlocked the door and rushed in.

"The closet's on fire," Gabrielle yelled. "Don't open it. There might be flames inside."

I ignored her and wrenched open the door. Adam staggered out, coughing and spluttering, and collapsed across the table. "No handle," he gasped. "No way out from the inside."

"What on earth?" Gabrielle demanded. "Was this some kind of prank?"

She went into the closet and reappeared with the smoke bomb, which she dropped into the metal wastebasket. "Are you totally out of your mind?" she yelled at Adam, who was still bending over the table, coughing and gasping for air. "This is so totally juvenile, I can't believe it. What were you trying to do, scare me—or were you trying to start a fire so that you'd have your own news story to write? Because either way, you were wasting your time."

Adam looked at her, his big dark eyes full of hurt. I couldn't stand to see him like this. Gabrielle didn't seem to notice that the guy couldn't breathe. She didn't seem to care that he could have been killed in that closet. I put my arm around him. "Come on, Adam. Let's get out of here," I said.

He let me lead him away.

"I really blew that, didn't I?" Adam asked in a cracked voice after he'd had a long drink at the drinking fountain outside the building. "I'm so stupid! I don't deserve a girl like Gabrielle."

I looked at him and something snapped. "*You* don't deserve her? Adam, what are you saying? *She's* the one who doesn't deserve *you*. She didn't even seem to notice that you couldn't breathe."

He shrugged. "Sure, she was mad at me. It looked like a stupid prank to her." He sank back onto the steps and buried his head in his hands. "Now I'll never have another chance with her. She'll see me as a juvenile idiot forever and ever."

"Adam, it wasn't your fault," I said. "I was equally to blame. We should have checked that you could get out of the closet again before we closed the door. So I should apologize to you for wrecking your chances."

He raised his head and managed a weak smile. "It's okay, Karen. I think I knew all along that I didn't really have a chance. I mean, can you see me as a superhero? Do I look the type?"

"Superman looked like Clark Kent a lot of the time," I said.

"You know, you're really nice," he said. "I've done all these dumb things and I've dragged you into them and never once have you told me I was making a fool of myself."

"What are friends for?" I said, trying to sound light and casual. He looked so depressed and fragile sitting there, his face streaked with smoke, his eyes still red and watering. All I wanted to do was sit next to him and wrap my arms around him. But I had to keep reminding myself that friends didn't do things like that—not if one friend was a boy and one was a girl.

13

Adam didn't come to school on Thursday. I wasn't sure if that was because he'd inhaled too much smoke and still felt sick or because he didn't want to risk facing Gabrielle ever again. A little of both, probably.

"I hope that's over now," Ginger said. "Honestly, Karen, I don't want to go through something like that again."

"Me neither, Karen," Roni said. "I felt like a total fool, babbling on and on to Brad. I can't even remember what I told him—something about a joint newspaper project with Oak Creek High. I just hope he hasn't called them and found out that there is no Oak Creek High newspaper."

"Don't worry, guys," I said. "It's definitely over.

There is no way that Adam will want to face Gabrielle again. I just wish he'd realize what a horrible person she is. She didn't even care that he was coughing and gasping. She just kept yelling at him."

"I wonder where Justine is?" Ginger asked. "She'll be late if she doesn't get here in a hurry, and she's already got two tardies this quarter."

She hadn't even finished speaking when we heard this loud "Yoo-hoo! Roni! Karen! Ginger!" We stood there with our mouths open, staring as Justine came down the hall toward us. I didn't recognize her at first. She was dressed in a black military uniform with lots of gold braid on it. It took me a second to realize it was a band uniform.

"Ta-da!" she yelled as she got close to us. "You are looking at Justine Craft, girl tuba player and newest member of the marching band."

"Justine!" Roni stammered. "They've really let you join? With your two notes?"

Justine didn't even blush. "I lied and told Mr. Healey I could play a scale. I figured I could fake it. If I don't know the note, I won't play it. But I'll be out there, marching with the band, only a few ranks behind Jeremy and his clarinet." Her face broke into a big smile. "I can't wait to see his face. You'll all have to come to the game tomorrow night and watch me."

"We wouldn't miss it for the world," Roni said, catching my eye as she closed her locker door.

On Friday I felt more nervous for Justine than she seemed to feel for herself.

"What about the routines?" I asked. I'd been to enough football games to know that the band did some fairly fancy stuff at halftime.

"Mr. Healey has told me what pieces are simple enough for me. And I'm at the back of the line. I just follow the person in front of me. Piece of cake."

I wished I had her confidence. If that had been me, playing an instrument in public for the first time, I'd have been a nervous wreck. Which is why the conservatory had been a waste of time for me, I decided. I got way too nervous when I had to play for people. Even in an orchestra, where I was one of a hundred musicians, I worried about screwing up and spoiling the whole thing. And if I had to play something as big as a tuba . . . I shuddered just thinking about it.

But Justine was excited, and I guess that was all that mattered. I'd be there for her—it would be fun to go to a football game with my friends, anyway.

When I went into chemistry, Adam was sitting there. He smiled at me shyly, but didn't say anything. I thought that maybe he'd rather be left alone for a while, so I didn't say anything either. But when I looked at him, he seemed so sad. Since he thought of me as his friend, I thought I should say something. After all, it was up to friends to make each other feel better when they were down.

"Hey, Adam," I whispered. "I'm going to the football game tonight with my friends. You want to come with us?"

He thought about it for a moment, then he nodded. "Sure, why not?"

"Meet you at six-thirty by the hot dog stand?" I asked.

He nodded again. "Okay."

Then he went back to something he was writing. I guess he was finishing up his column. Brad would be on his case if he didn't get it by the end of today.

Adam was still sitting there scribbling away when the bell rang. I left him to it. I didn't see him again until I went to meet him before the football game.

"Hi," I said. "Are you ready to watch the team massacre Scottsdale?"

"Sure," he said quietly. We walked together in silence toward the bleachers where I'd left Roni and Ginger.

"Karen," he blurted suddenly. "I want you to know I've quit the newspaper. I sent in my resignation this afternoon."

"Adam, why?"

"That's pretty obvious, isn't it? I made the world's biggest fool of myself. Gabrielle's never going to let me forget that. I couldn't stand being in the same room with her every week."

"But Adam, you're a terrific writer," I said. "You're one of the best writers on the whole newspaper. And you love it. You can't give it up just because of what one girl thinks of you."

"That one girl is the news editor," he said. "I get the feeling that if she doesn't like someone, he's dead meat."

"Brad's the editor, and he still thinks you're okay."

"Gabrielle's probably told him what happened by now. I'm sure she's told half the school what happened. I bet everyone's laughing at me behind my back."

"So let them laugh," I said angrily. "You've got to learn to stand up for yourself, Adam. You have to decide that it's your life and nobody else is going to run it for you. When I decided to quit the music conservatory, it was the scariest thing I've ever done in my life. I'd never disobeyed my parents before—not when it came to something major, anyway. But I knew I couldn't go on doing something that wasn't right for me. They're still making my life miserable, but I don't care." I put my hand

159

on his shoulder. "Gabrielle might not be too easy to work with for a while, but you've got to learn not to care too . . . not if writing is what you really want to do."

"I don't know," he said hesitantly.

"Are you going to let one crummy girl ruin all your career plans?" I demanded. "Do you want to look back when you're old and say 'I could have been a journalist but some girl stopped me'?"

He grinned. "It does sound pretty dumb when you put it like that. But it's too late now. I left my resignation in Brad's office this afternoon."

"Maybe he hasn't found it yet," I said. "There's a chance he went straight to the JV football game. I saw him in the office pretty early. Why don't we go up there now and see if we can find it?"

He looked at me nervously. "You really think we should?"

"Answer me this, Adam Bateman," I said. "Do you want to work on this newspaper or not?"

"I want to," he said. "Especially if you're there to keep me going."

"I'll be there."

"Then let's go," he said. He grabbed my hand and dragged me forward. "I'm so glad you were here tonight, Karen," he yelled as we ran across the twilit school yard. "I was feeling so depressed and so mad at myself. I didn't think I could face the world ever again. My mother had to force me to come to school today. But I'm glad she did."

We found a door that was still open. Our feet clattered through the empty halls.

"I just hope we're not too late," Adam said. We were halfway to the office when he stopped. "We are too late," he said. "There's a light on. Somebody's working in there."

"If it's Brad, tell him you were depressed and you made a mistake. He'll understand."

"I hope so," he said. "If it's Gabrielle, we'll just turn around and creep back downstairs again."

We inched closer. The door was open and light was spilling out into the hall. When we were only a few feet away, we heard Gabrielle's voice resound sharply. "What are you doing here?"

Adam leaped a mile, but it was obvious that she wasn't speaking to us. Almost instantly a guy's deep voice answered. "What do you think, Gaby? Trying to get you alone. Are you playing hard to get or what?"

Adam glanced at me. We crept closer.

"I told you, Steve. I'm not interested, okay? So stop following me like this."

"Aw, come on, Gaby, you know you really like me. I've seen you looking at me in class. I know you've got the hots for me."

"In your dreams," Gabrielle snapped. "Now

would you get out of here and leave me alone? I have stuff to finish up."

"Not until you give me a kiss, Gaby."

"Are you crazy? Get your hands off me." We could hear the sounds of scuffling. Gabrielle's voice sounded high and tense now. "Let go of me, Steve. Stop it right now, do you hear me?"

Before I could grab Adam, he darted forward. He stepped into the doorway. "You heard the lady. Get your hands off her," he said.

Steve laughed. "What are you going to do about it, kid?"

"I'm warning you," Adam said, and his voice sounded calm and strong. "I've got a black belt in karate."

This made Steve laugh even harder. *Oh, Adam,* I thought, *you really do say dumb things sometimes. Now you're going to get massacred.* I stood just outside the door, ready to rush in and rescue him.

"You'd better get out of here while you still can," Adam said.

"Ooh, I'm really scared," Steve taunted. He let go of Gabrielle and stepped forward to give Adam a shove. "What do you think you could do to me, runt?"

One minute Steve was reaching out to push Adam, the next he was flying through the air. I was so astonished that I didn't think about getting out of the way. Steve did a complete flip in midair, and when his feet came flying in my direction I went sprawling backward. I hit the wall across the hall as Steve landed with a thump on the hall floor.

"Sorry, but you asked for it," Adam said.

Steve scrambled to his feet as Gabrielle laughed and clapped. "You went flying, Mr. Macho. Should we call you Peter Pan now?"

"Shut up," Steve growled. "So I slipped. They shouldn't polish this floor so much." He glared at Adam. "Next time I'll be ready for you, creep."

"Anytime," Adam said. He sounded totally cool. Steve looked at him long and hard, then swaggered off down the hall.

Only then did Adam notice me leaning against the wall, holding my side where Steve's feet had struck me.

"Are you okay, Karen?"

I nodded. "I think so."

"You really do have a black belt in karate," Gabrielle said in an astonished voice.

Adam blushed modestly. "I've been taking lessons since I was four, but I've never had to use it before. It's good to know it really works, especially when I need it to. I'm so glad I was able to save you, Gabrielle."

Gabrielle was staring at him as if she'd just noticed him for the first time. "That was amazing," she said. "I've never seen anything like that outside of the movies. He went flying. Incredible. Steve Garcia—Mr. Macho—and you threw him on his back. I love it."

"It's easy when you know how," Adam said. He was still trying to sound modest, but he was looking a little like Mr. Macho himself now.

Gabrielle came over to him. "Look, Adam, I'm sorry I yelled at you the other day. You're a totally sweet guy to save me like that. You're a real hero." She put her hand on his arm. "Listen, my car's outside. I'm kind of shaken up after that creepy guy grabbed me, and I guess you are, too. You want to go get a coffee someplace?"

"Uh, sure," Adam said.

"I . . . should be getting back to my friends, then," I said awkwardly. "They'll be wondering where I am. Have fun, Adam."

I started to walk away, not looking back. I couldn't believe the last five minutes. We couldn't have scripted it better if we'd tried. Adam really was a hero and Gabrielle really had been swept off her feet. Totally amazing . . . almost too incredible to believe. Only the dull ache in my side where Steve's feet had caught me told me that it was all true.

I kept walking down the stairs and out into the warm evening air. It was almost dark now. I could hear the band playing. That must mean that the game was about to start. *So that's over,* I thought. *Adam and Gabrielle live happily ever after.* Who would have thought it? Maybe it was true that blondes did have more fun. Maybe I was too blah for guys to be interested in me as anything more than a friend. . . .

I was halfway across the yard when I heard feet running behind me. "Karen, wait up," a breathless voice called.

I turned around and saw Adam standing there.

"What are you doing here?" I asked. "I thought you were going for coffee with Gabrielle. You'd better not keep her waiting."

"I told her thanks but no thanks," he said.

"Why?"

He shrugged. "I don't like coffee very much."

"Adam! That was your big chance, and you blew it?"

He shook his head. "You were right all along, Karen. I was living in a fantasy world. Gabrielle was always out of my league, always will be out of my league. I think I always knew it, too, but I was just too dumb to admit it."

"But she was really impressed tonight. You were her hero, Adam. Just like you dreamed."

"I know," he said. "For just a moment I really felt like a hero."

"But?"

"I couldn't get this picture out of my mind of you walking away down the hall when I hadn't even bothered to find out if you'd really hurt yourself. I told Gabrielle that I should go check on you first, and you know what she said? She said, 'Forget it. Why worry about her? She's nobody.' And suddenly it was just like someone had taken off these blinders I'd been wearing. I looked at her and I knew that she just used people and she didn't care about anyone except herself. And I knew something else, too. . . ."

His eyes were glowing in the lights from the football field.

"What?" I asked.

"That I really cared a lot about you. As I ran after you, I found myself thinking, 'If that Steve guy hurt her, I'll break every bone in his body!'"

"Adam, you're getting very violent suddenly," I said, laughing nervously because I couldn't believe this was happening either. "Is this new, improved Adam Bateman going to last?"

He smiled at me. "Just tell me that you're okay and I can go back to being my old wimpy self. If that's what you'd rather have."

"I'm okay, and I think I'd rather have the old Adam. I just can't take all the excitement of being around Rambo."

He gave an embarrassed smile. "I'm not very

comfortable being Rambo. I was totally scared that my karate wouldn't work."

"But it did. You were amazing, Adam. Why didn't you ever mention that you had a black belt?"

He grinned again. "I'll let you in on a little secret. I only have a brown belt. That's one below black, but black sounds more impressive, doesn't it?"

"It sure impressed Gabrielle. Are you sure you don't want to live out your fantasy and go on a date with her?"

He shook his head. "I'd be terrified of knocking over the coffee or offering her sugar when she's on a diet. I think I'd rather stick with you, if you don't mind. I'm comfortable around you."

"Gee, that's about the most flattering thing anyone has ever said to me," I teased. "Good old comfortable Karen. I feel like a pair of old bedroom slippers."

"I didn't mean it like that," he said. "I just meant that I don't have to try and impress you all the time. We get along so well together. You even know what I'm thinking. That's pretty special, isn't it?"

I nodded. "I guess it is."

"And we started out as friends. That's the right way to start, isn't it?" He took hold of my hands. He was standing very close to me, his eyes smiling into mine. "Meeting you was the best thing that ever happened to me, Karen. Do you think we can go on being friends, maybe even be more than friends?"

"We can try," I said.

"Great," he said. "In that case I've got something to ask you."

"What?" I asked tenderly.

"Could we go get a hot dog before the game? I'm starving."

"Adam, you say the most romantic things." I laughed.

He squeezed my hand. "I'll say romantic things later if you like, but right now I sure could do with a hot dog—no, make that a chili dog."

"Typical boy," I muttered to myself as he led me across to the hot dog stand.

We found Roni and Ginger just after the game had started. They looked at Adam, still holding my hand, then at me. Roni raised an eyebrow. I grinned. "Tell you later," I whispered as we squeezed onto the bleachers beside her. Adam put his arm around my shoulders. It felt great. It wasn't like the moment I knew I had fallen in love with James. It wasn't like my crush on Damien. There were no fireworks going off and there was no feeling that my heart might explode any second. It was a warm, comfortable feeling—I knew just what Adam meant—and I liked it.

We sat close together, his arm around me and his knee touching mine, until halftime. There was a great burst of music and the band marched out onto the field. They looked really impressive in their uniforms with the lights sparkling from the gold braid and brass instruments. It wasn't hard to pick out Justine, or at least, to pick out the tuba. Justine was totally hidden within it. I thought I heard a sound like a dying elephant, so I guessed she was trying to play and march at the same time.

The band marched smartly to the center of the field and then wheeled off left and right. At least, most of the band wheeled off. One tuba player kept on going straight. There was a murmur from the crowd and then some giggles and then everyone was laughing and calling out. This made Justine finally stop. She looked around, saw the rest of the band disappearing down the field, and started to run to catch up. Kids were yelling out at her as she tried to run, still carrying the monster tuba. Then suddenly she must have caught her foot, because she tripped and went sprawling, flinging the tuba off her just before she went down hard on the turf.

Roni, Ginger, and I leaped instantly from our seats and fought our way down to the field. But before we could get there, someone else ran to her. It was Jeremy. He darted out from the clarinet section and ran across to her. He was kneeling beside her by the time we made our way across the field.

Justine was sobbing so hard, she didn't even see us coming. "I've made such a fool of myself again," she gasped between sobs. "I'll have to transfer out. I'll never be able to face anyone again."

"Don't worry about it," Jeremy said. "It could happen to anyone."

"Oh, right. How many other people do you think have ever marched the wrong way?" Justine demanded.

"Me," Jeremy said. "I did at my old school. I was concentrating so hard on the music that I didn't bother to look up. When I did look up, the rest of the band was at the other end of the field. So I know how it feels."

"You do?" Justine stopped sobbing and was gazing up at him.

"It feels like the end of the world," Jeremy said. "But it's really no big deal. Football players make mistakes all the time. They drop the ball, they fumble, they get sacked, and nobody holds it against them. So come on, Justine. Here, take my hand."

Justine reached out and let Jeremy pull her to her feet.

"There. Are you okay?" he asked gently. Justine

nodded. "Then let's get back to the band," he said.

Justine shook her head. "You go. I don't belong there. I'm useless at music. I only started playing this stupid tuba to impress you."

"Me?" Jeremy sounded totally surprised. "You wanted to impress me?"

"Yes, you idiot. I wanted you to forget about Karen and notice me."

"I had no idea," Jeremy mumbled. Which shows you how clueless some guys can be. "Justine. I don't know what to say. I'm flattered. A great-looking girl like you? Wow. But why did you choose the tuba? It's such a hard instrument."

"Because they didn't have a tuba player in the band."

Jeremy smiled. "Justine, you're funny. I'll help you learn an instrument if you like. You could try the piccolo. That's not too hard."

"It's okay," Justine said. "I think I've learned that it doesn't work to pretend to be something you're not just to attract a guy. I like listening to music, but I'll never be a musician."

"I like listening to music too," Jeremy said. "There's an outdoor concert tomorrow night. Do you want to go with me?"

"I'd love to," Justine said.

"Great," Jeremy said. He turned to me. "I hope you don't mind, Karen."

171

Jeremy really wasn't so bad after all. I just hadn't given him a chance to prove himself. But I'd have more time to get to know him later if he and Justine became friends. I glanced around and Adam was standing behind me. "That's okay," I said. "I think I've got other plans." I took Adam's hand as we made our way back off the field.

Read these other groovesome Boyfriend Club titles

1. GINGER'S FIRST KISS

Ginger, Justine, Karen and Roni start at their huge new school. Join the foursome as they embark on their adventures.

2. RONI'S DREAM BOY

Roni sees her ideal boy at the Boyfriend Club seance. And he really exists. But not only is he the most popular boy in school, he also has a girlfriend. What can Roni do?

3. KAREN'S PERFECT MATCH

The nerds invent a computer program to match the girls to their ideal date. Karen's is in the orchestra with her. But why does she run the other way every time they meet?

4. QUEEN JUSTINE

Justine upsets her friends by joining the snobbiest club in school, the Kestrels. Will their friendships survive, particularly as Justine expects the club to serve food at the Kestrel's dance?